"*What was that all about?*"

Justine was breathing hard, her glasses askew.

"What?" Clayton asked innocently, his eyes dancing. He reached up and plucked the glasses from her nose.

"Kissing me like that! What makes you think you can—"

"We're getting married, aren't we?" His eyes held hers.

She nodded slowly and let her breath out.

"So? It's settled, then." He reached into his pocket and casually pulled out a jeweller's box. Without the slightest fuss, he opened it, took out a ring and slid it onto her left ring finger.

She stared down at the square-cut diamond, plainly set in a wide platinum band. It gleamed like the clearest, purest mountain water—and it fit perfectly.

"Very good, Justine," he murmured, his eyes narrowed. "Just the right amount of surprise and gratitude. You should be able to handle this job perfectly. And just remember—" his eyes flashed wickedly "—kissing me is part of your job now, O'Malley. Better get used to it."

Dear Reader,

October is a very special month at Silhouette Romance. We're celebrating the most precious love of all . . . a child's love. Our editors have selected five heartwarming stories that feature happy-ever-afters with a family touch—*Home for Thanksgiving* by Suzanne Carey, *And Daddy Makes Three* by Anne Peters, *Casey's Flyboy* by Vivian Leiber, *Paper Marriage* by Judith Bowen and *Beloved Stranger* by Peggy Webb.

But that's not all! We're also continuing our WRITTEN IN THE STARS series. This month we're proud to present one of the most romantic heroes in the zodiac—the Libra man—in Patricia Ellis's *Pillow Talk*.

I hope you enjoy this month's stories, and in the months to come, watch for Silhouette Romance novels by your all-time favorites, including Diana Palmer, Brittany Young, Annette Broadrick and many others.

The authors and editors of Silhouette Romance books strive to bring you the best of romance fiction, stories that capture the laughter, the tears—the sheer joy—of falling in love. Let us know if we've succeeded. We'd love to hear from you!

Happy Reading,

Valerie Susan Hayward
Senior Editor

JUDITH BOWEN

Paper
Marriage

Silhouette **Romance**
Published by Silhouette Books New York
America's Publisher of Contemporary Romance

To my editors, with respect and affection:
To Tara, for throwing the lifeline;
To Paula, for hauling me aboard

SILHOUETTE BOOKS
300 E. 42nd St., New York, N.Y. 10017

PAPER MARRIAGE

ISBN: 0-373-08823-X

First Silhouette Books printing October 1991

Printed in the U.S.A.

JUDITH BOWEN

met her husband when they were editing competing newspapers in British Columbia, and they were married in Gibraltar. She has enjoyed raising sheep and children in Fraser Valley, and still spins wool, knits, weaves and puts up dozens of jars of preserves and pickles every year. Her interests include reading, regional cookery, volunteer work, gardening and, of course, writing romances.

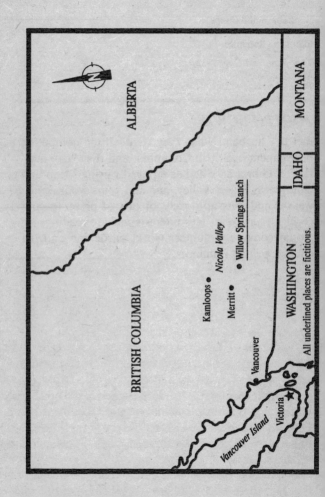

Chapter One

"I want those children and I'll do anything I have to do to get them."

The man silhouetted against the big windows stared broodingly down at the traffic fourteen stories below, restlessness evident in every line of his long, lean body.

"Anything?" The lawyer's voice was tentative. What in the world did Clayton Truscott have in mind?

"Anything!" The man at the window turned suddenly and strode into the center of the room, stopping in front of the polished walnut desk to throw a folded paper onto the shiny surface. He jammed his hands in the pockets of his black cowhide jacket, rocking slightly forward on the balls of his feet, the unconscious move of a natural athlete ready for anything. "The details are all there, John."

The blue-green eyes were colder than the lawyer had ever seen them, and he'd known his client since they were boys together growing up in the rolling grasslands of the

Nicola Valley many years before. The dark frown softened slightly, but Clayton Truscott's grim smile didn't
touch his eyes. And when he spoke, his voice was low
and hard and angry.

"I need a woman, my friend, and it's going to be your
job to find me the right one."

Justine O'Malley nearly choked on the orange juice
she'd just poured for herself before picking up the
kitchen phone on the third ring. She cradled the re-
ceiver on one shoulder while she hastily set down the
glass and wiped her chin with the tail of the oversize
man's cotton shirt she favored as nighttime attire.

"You're kidding! Six months? It's perfect! In fact, it
almost sounds too good to be true." She bit down on her
lower lip as she listened to Sonia, her roommate and legal assistant or something-or-other at a big downtown
law firm.

"It's all very hush-hush," Sonia went on in a guarded
tone that made Justine wonder if her friend was supposed to be passing along the latest scuttlebutt at Stusiak, Stusiak, and Acorn, "but I thought of you as soon
as Charlotte told me about it." Charlotte, Justine gathered, was another legal something-or-other and it was
her boss, John Stusiak, who was looking for a short-
term nanny for a mystery client. "Shall I tell Charlotte
you're interested?"

Interested? You bet she was! Justine hung up the
phone and frowned slightly as she ran an impatient hand
through her shoulder-length curls. Could this be the pot
of gold she'd been dreaming about? There was no question, she couldn't stay much longer at Peter Rabbit, the
play school where she'd worked for the past two years.
Something had to give.

Not that Justine O'Malley didn't like children. In fact, she loved children. That is what had kept her at Peter Rabbit for so long, in what she knew was basically a dead-end job. That is why she'd changed careers after training as a nurse. She'd wanted to spend time with healthy, happy children after the pain she'd felt nursing little broken bodies in the pediatrics ward. That's why, at the ripe old age of twenty-six, Justine knew she needed a switch.

It was now or never. If she didn't strike out on her own, open her own play school soon—she had all the qualifications—what would she be saying to herself in another two years' time? You blew it, girl, you should have struck while the iron was hot. While the Mac-Allister place was for sale.

But it all came down to money. It always did. Justine sighed as she crossed to the sink.

"Yech!"

Sonia had left the sink full of last night's dishes—as usual—before dashing out to work this morning. Justine balanced her plate precariously on a pile of used cutlery and walked into the living room they shared. Empty beer cans, cigarette butts. She wrinkled her nose with distaste. That was another thing. Roommates! She loved her scatty roommate dearly, but was she ever going to be able to afford to get out on her own?

MacAllister House could be her dream come true. Her own play school on the main floor, an apartment upstairs, the slower cadences of a small-town life again. But where would she get the money to buy and restore a decaying heritage building? She had some savings, scratched together over the past couple of years, but not anywhere near enough to buy the rambling, old, three-story Victorian.

Mostly, Justine wanted to run a play school along her own lines. She wanted a school filled with play and fun and cooperation and with hardly any so-called structured learning at all. How she was coming to hate the term "educational play." All it meant was push, push, push to a whole generation of children rushed into get-ahead situations by parents obsessed with their own needs over the needs of their children....

Oh, what's the use, Justine thought, pushing back her heavy hair with both hands again. It just makes you mad thinking about it.

She'd never save enough from her meager salary—not in a million years. But if she could get her hands on a sizable lump sum somehow...maybe use her savings to take an option on the place, keep the current tenants for a while. A six-month, one-shot position.... What did she have to lose?

Five days later, neatly clad in a businesslike navy skirt, matching jacket and white lawn blouse, discreetly feminine but buttoned tightly right to the top. Justine sat, ankles primly crossed, in the plush reception area of Stusiak, Stusiak and Acorn. She took a deep breath, then another. Relax, girl. You can do it. If only the mysterious client is as impressed with your qualifications as the lawyer had been on the telephone.

Justine cast a quick sidelong glance at the other woman in the reception area. Tall, svelte, elegantly dressed in a jade green silk suit, pale blond hair swept into a shining roll at the back of her head. Justine knew what price that apparently careless elegance. She'd struggled with her own chestnut mane for fully half an hour this morning trying to force it into some sort of smooth domesticity. Calm, serious, very capable. That was the impression she wanted to make on her potential employer.

Had she been wrong? That blonde was going to be difficult to top if Mr. X was the kind of gentleman who preferred blondes. Her heart sank, slightly.

She pushed up her glasses. They felt awkward—still. How in heaven's name did the half of the world that wore spectacles manage? Hers were plain glass, slightly tinted, large and horn-rimmed, an impulse purchase she'd made when she got the call from Stusiak's office telling her she was on the shortlist for the job.

"Your qualifications are excellent, Miss O'Malley," the lawyer had said when he'd phoned to set up the interview. She hadn't met him; she had only filled out a long form, given to her by an extremely competent assistant, that asked for all kinds of information regarding qualifications and character references. "I think my client will be especially pleased with your nursing background. You see," the lawyer had hesitated, as though perhaps wondering just how much he should reveal to this candidate "—my client's, er—the children are fairly young, five and three, and the boy, the elder, has asthma. Oh, it's nothing too serious," he said quickly, in response to her small murmur of sympathy, "but, well, it's certainly a point in your favor."

He'd asked her several more questions about her background, her family, then had startled her with his next question.

"Have you a fiancé, Miss O'Malley? Any special man in your life?"

It was an odd question, she'd thought at the time, but she'd answered smoothly, "No, Mr. Stusiak, I am completely unattached."

"Very good. Because, you see—" his voice lowered, confidentially "—I may as well tell you I'm going to recommend you for the position."

Justine felt her heart soar in her chest and she swallowed hard, not wanting him to know just how desperately she wanted this job. "My client wants rather more than a nanny for the children. He—well, if he thinks you're suitable he will explain the extra duties to you himself. It's, uh, an extremely confidential matter—I'm sorry to be so awkward, Miss O'Malley."

"It's quite all right." She had smiled a little to herself. Of course, it *would* be extremely confidential. Wasn't that, after all, the raison d'être of the entire legal profession?

"Good. Will two o'clock Friday suit you? In my office? I've convinced my client to interview the applicants and make the final choice himself."

He'd laughed, a rather too-hearty forced sort of laugh, Justine remembered thinking at the time. Convinced him? What kind of man would let someone else—a lawyer—choose a nanny for his children?

Justine's reverie was interrupted by the low tones of the receptionist.

"Miss Stillman?" The blond woman rose and disappeared down the hall. Just then the previous interviewee appeared, looking like the cat who had swallowed the canary, buxom, slightly disheveled, her eyes aglow. Well, Justine thought, she certainly looks pleased with herself. Blonde, too.

She didn't have long to wait. Within ten minutes the elegant Miss Stillman returned, heels clicking angrily on the hardwood floor. She collected her coat and left, a thin smile pasted to her face. Strike two, Justine thought, getting to her feet and nervously smoothing her skirt, wondering for the umpteenth time if she should have worn her beige linen, if the sprightly little peplum on the back of her navy jacket was too... well, too sprightly. This interview was absolutely crucial.

Chin high, Miss O'Malley, she said to herself, and pushed up the glasses again. She followed the receptionist down the hall and took a deep breath just before entering the conference room.

It was a fairly large room. A big polished desk stood near the far wall with a couple of upholstered chairs positioned in front of it. There was another seating area, partially screened and shadowed by an arrangement of plants, nearer the large, long windows that let natural light flood the room. Beyond the windows was an unobstructed view of the North Shore mountains, the Lions rearing their snowy heads above the entire city of Vancouver and its inner harbor. It was a magnificent view, and in this city, where the exact quality of a view or lack of one was neatly measured and marketed, Justine knew the price per square foot in this lawyer's quarters would match that magnificence.

"Miss O'Malley?" A pleasant-looking man of slightly above medium height was advancing to meet her. Justine smiled brilliantly. She was ridiculously relieved to find her interlocutor so, well, so ordinary. Heavens! All this mysterious buildup to what was after all just another job interview. "Please sit down. Would you like some coffee?"

"No, thank you." He nodded, and walked around to take the chair behind the desk. She could see he had a copy of her curriculum vitae in front of him. Was this the lawyer? Or Mr. X? He hadn't introduced himself, which seemed a bit odd, but that could mean he was the mystery man. He probably wouldn't identify himself until he'd picked her for the job. Good grief! Why hadn't he just worn a mask and have done with it? She felt a tiny bubble of laughter rising and firmly squelched it.

"Miss O'Malley, your qualifications are impressive. I understand you're a registered nurse as well as having a degree in early-childhood education." He raised one sandy eyebrow and smiled. She nodded. Then he placed the fingers of his hands together, carefully, tip to tip, and leaned back in his chair. "I wonder if you'd mind telling me just why you're interested in this particular job?" Had she been mistaken, or had he flashed a quick glance toward the window area?

"It's quite simple, sir. It's a question of money." She'd decided to be completely frank; after all, with her qualifications it did seem a bit unusual that she'd be seeking an interim job like this, not a career position. His glance shifted again, toward the far side of the room. Justine felt the tiny hairs at the back of her neck prickle, as though sensing an unseen presence. "You see, I've always wanted to open a play school of my own, on my own premises and I've found it a difficult goal to accomplish on my salary as a play-school teacher. You probably know we're generally an underpaid lot."

She smiled and he grinned back, quick to respond. She felt the usual sort of friendly appreciation most men had for a pretty woman from him, and it was a pleasant, comfortable feeling. But something—she couldn't put her finger on it exactly—was not quite right. "I suppose I see this job as a means to an end. So—?" She shrugged and raised her hands, palms up, in a small gesture of helplessness.

"So a term of six months, or thereabouts, suits you?"

"Yes. Very well."

"And money—?" He named a substantial figure. Justine's eyes widened slightly. "Of course, living expenses and all other costs would be met. And there would be a substantial bonus upon satisfactory completion of the term."

"Sir?"

"Yes?" He looked inquiringly at her.

"I understand it's not, well, an *ordinary* nanny position—?" She hesitated. The money offered was beyond her wildest dreams—enough to buy MacAllister House easily—but with money like that there had to be a catch somewhere. And the catch must be in the mysterious aspects of the job not yet spelled out. "You—you haven't elaborated."

"No. I haven't." The man behind the desk looked over to the far corner of the room again, toward the half-shadowed seating area, and this time Justine followed his glance. At first she didn't see the other man, then she turned right around to stare at him.

Who in the world was this, slouched down deep on the sofa, long legs stretched in front of him, a black—was it a Stetson?—hat pulled low over his eyes? The light was behind him and she could barely make him out although she knew he could see her clearly. Denims encased his long legs, a well-cut dark green shirt covered the broad, muscular torso and his arms were crossed, a gold watch gleaming dully on his left wrist.

Ridiculously, the watch stood out in her mind, as though some part of her registered the very expensive instrument as being at odds somehow with the jeans and the well-worn leather jacket. As she watched, incredulous, she saw him nod, ever so slightly. And with her intuition, more than anything, she felt the tension seep out of the man at the desk.

"Ask her to stand up, John," came the deep voice, almost a growl. "And take that ridiculous jacket off."

The other man repeated the instructions, much more politely, but Justine could tell he was a little embarrassed by the abrupt request. Just who was this man anyway? She stood, removed her jacket and curtsied slightly in the stranger's direction. She still couldn't see his face clearly, and suddenly she resented that fact.

"Walk this way, Miss O'Malley. Please."

The request—order, she corrected herself—was only slightly more polite. Justine could hear the derision in the slow drawl. Her insolent curtsy had not gone unnoticed.

With a sudden movement the man got up and in a couple of strides was beside her, his hand on her chin, tilting it up, his eyes—a curious blue-green she noticed vaguely, as though in a dream—narrowed on her face. Instinctive fear must have flickered in her eyes, for he suddenly dropped her chin and nodded, mockingly.

"Could you come over here, Miss O'Malley? By the window? I want a good look at you."

Justine threw a furious glance at the man at the desk. Why was he just sitting there, looking extremely interested? While this—this cowboy—looked her over like a prime bit of horseflesh he might—or might not—be interested in bidding on?

At the window, the man stopped and turned her toward him again. Justine felt a brief flash of hysteria as she looked up and met those disconcerting eyes regarding her so intently. She closed hers briefly as his hand moved up slowly to reach behind her head, then she felt his fingers fumble in her hair and grasp the pins that secured her smooth chignon. With one deft, surprisingly gentle movement, he'd removed the clips and her hair fell slowly about her shoulders. Her eyes snapped open. This was outrageous!

The man in front of her, smelling faintly of clean male skin and plain soap, worn leather and...something else—the fresh, chill scent of wide-open spaces—but that *had* to be her imagination, she thought wildly—did not take any notice of her suddenly stiffened posture. He turned her face toward the window with hard fingers, then reached up and removed her glasses. For a moment wide tawny eyes gazed deep into blue-green, the desert meeting the sea, and Justine felt something flutter deep inside her, at her midriff, just where the ancients had said the soul lived. Then it was gone.

His eyes were hard as stone, and his mouth tightened. She could see the faint black stubble on the square jaw, as though he hadn't bothered to shave yet today, and the firm lips, very near her, thinned with some emotion she couldn't quite fathom. Was it contempt?

He stepped back and looked her over with quick practised eyes, frowning, taking in the fashionable but modest lines of the suit that failed to disguise the feminine curves, the slim legs, the trim ankles and feet in navy pumps. With her glasses off and her hair down, she was an entirely different creature.

He stared at her for a long hard moment, the black lashes framing the beautiful eyes, squinting almost, as though to blur her image, a deep frown on the handsome face. Then he turned abruptly away.

"Well, John, what do you think?" He strolled casually toward the desk. Justine was left standing by the window, her mouth practically agape.

"Well, her qualifications are excellent and—" the other began, but the tall stranger cut him off abruptly.

"Yeah. She'll do." He resettled the Stetson, pulling it down firmly over the thick black hair, longish in the back, nearly over his collar. "Well, I'm off. I can tell you this has been a hell of a nuisance coming right in the middle of branding season, John, and I ought to damn well fire you for dragging me down." He reached one hand up to massage the back of his neck wearily, but Justine could detect a trace of humor in the deep voice. These men knew each other well.

"It was that or me sending a shortlist up to the ranch," the man at the desk said. "And I knew you wouldn't stand for that."

"Yeah. Well." He flexed his broad shoulders casually and Justine could see the smooth play of hard muscle under the supple black leather. "I need a couple hours' sleep and a shower now that you've got me here. You'll take care of the details?" The man he'd called John nodded, a pleased smile on his face.

Then, as though suddenly remembering her presence, the other man turned and gave her a smile, a lazy crooked grin that did strange things to her heart, already hammering as it was. "I'll see you later, Miss O'Malley. John will fill you in." And he nodded and turned to go to the door.

A sudden panic gripped Justine. This was the most bizarre job interview she'd ever been through. What was happening? What in the world had she gotten herself into?

"Just a minute!" She stepped into the center of the room. The stranger turned, one dark eyebrow raised in inquiry, a half smile on his lips.

"Yes?"

"Who are you anyway? What's going on here? I thought—"

"I'm Clayton Truscott, Miss O'Malley." He gave her a mock bow, tipping his hat. "I'm your new boss." And on that astonishing note, he closed the door behind him.

Justine turned, her shock and outrage at the way she'd been set up for this interview—for that's what had happened, she knew—mingled with her sudden urge to shout with joy. The job was hers! Strike three—it was a home run for MacAllister Play School and Justine O'Malley! She neither demanded an explanation nor danced a quick mad jig, though. Her knees felt suddenly weak and she sank gratefully into the soft chair in front of the desk. Somehow, just then, it seemed the best thing to do.

"So you—you must be the lawyer?" Her voice reflected her bewilderment.

"Yes. John Stusiak," he said and came around to offer her his hand again. He squeezed hers reassuringly then leaned casually against the desk, arms crossed. "I'm sorry about this, I really am. But it's the only way I could convince Clayton to cooperate. He just would not agree to interview the candidates, nor did he want anyone but the successful candidate to know who he was."

Who was this Clayton Truscott anyway, to merit such consideration, she thought with annoyance? Still, he was paying the piper.... And the job she'd just been offered paid very, very well indeed. "I see." But, in fact, she didn't.

"Er, about the position, Mr. Stusiak—" She had recovered from her initial surprise and realized that even though the job was apparently hers for the taking, she still didn't know—really—what it entailed.

"I know, I know—" The lawyer stared at her for a moment, seeming to register finally the stubborn note in her voice. "Clayton wants to meet you at his hotel—the Hawthorne—at seven tonight. Relax, have dinner, get to know you a little. And he'd like to go over everything with you then, in detail."

"I'd—I'd really rather know now, sir. If you don't mind." Justine was firm. She picked up her bag and suit jacket and stood, waiting for his response. After all, there was every possibility that she wouldn't be meeting Clayton Truscott for dinner at all—not if she couldn't live with the mysterious other duties, whatever they were.

Stusiak shrugged. "You're quite right." Then he turned and walked behind the desk. "Sit down, Miss O'Malley. I'll explain."

Chapter Two

Four hours later, battling the early-evening traffic across the Burrard Street Bridge, Justine was having serious second thoughts about the evening ahead.

She bit her lip and glanced in the rearview mirror, apologizing silently to the little Volkswagen as she gunned the engine, skipped into the outside lane and brought her car to a stop at the red light. Ah, ten more minutes. She sighed, craning her neck to get a glimpse of the big neon clock on the side of the Pattison Building. She might just make it.

The Hawthorne on Hornby. It was a midsize establishment—old, exquisitely refurbished by its new owner and catering to an exclusive clientele. Distinctly posh. Somehow she couldn't imagine a hard-edged cowboy like Clayton Truscott among the Queen Anne bric-a-brac. But then Clayton Truscott was clearly no ordinary cowboy. In fact, he was shaping up to be a very dark horse indeed.

She was meeting him for dinner in the Wildwood Room, known for its French cuisine. Justine had refused an offer by Stusiak to have his client pick her up or send a taxi for her. Things were moving along altogether too quickly as it was and she wanted the independence of her own wheels. This was no ordinary date.

The lawyer had been blunt.

"To tell you the truth, Miss O'Malley, Clayton Truscott isn't really looking for a nanny in the usual sense of the word," he'd confessed. "Elsie Grant, the Truscott housekeeper, has practically brought up the children single-handedly as it is. And she's done a fine job, in the circumstances." Justine's brow had creased slightly. Circumstances? The situation sounded very odd and unhappy, particularly for the children. Where was their mother? Why had they wanted a nanny?

"As a matter of fact, they're not even Clayton's own children—they're his niece and nephew. Orphaned, that is. Clayton's brother and his wife never spent much time at the ranch and they were killed in a plane crash a couple of months ago. In Antigua." He raised his eyebrows inquiringly, as though perhaps expecting that she'd heard of the tragedy. Justine shook her head.

"Clayton wants the children—naturally, they are his only brother's children—but their grandparents on their mother's side are fighting him for custody. Clayton thinks they want them for their own ulterior reasons and he's dead set against them succeeding—"

"Just a minute—" Justine's brow was furrowed as she concentrated, trying to follow the situation. "I presume there's a Mrs. Clayton Truscott somewhere in this—"

"No." The lawyer regarded her intently. "That's just it. There's not." He continued to look at her speculatively for a moment, eyes narrowed. "Clayton's not married, and I don't suppose I need to tell you how the courts would regard him as a potential father." Justine shook her head, perplexed. Where did she fit into all this?

"The point is, Miss O'Malley, Clayton needs a wife, to prove to the court that he's able to provide a stable family climate for the children, until he gets legal custody." The lawyer paused, waited expectantly.

"You mean, he's going to..." she said slowly, as comprehension dawned. She swallowed hard and began again. "He—"

"Yes. He needs a wife. Temporarily, of course. And he's decided on you for the job."

Justine still hadn't absorbed it. Not completely. A wife for hire? To dupe the courts? It was unconscionable! It didn't matter how much money he was offering! What about the children, where did their needs fit into this— this preposterous plot?

There was a squeal of tires from a car in the inner lane as it sped past and the driver behind her leaned on his horn. The light had gone green. Justine let out the clutch, peering ahead for a parking spot. What luck! There was a sedan pulling out of its space across the street from the Hawthorne and she expertly wheeled the little car into it.

She glanced quickly in the mirror, eyes wide with anticipation, clear skin glowing. She'd only worn a little makeup, just enough to heighten her own healthy coloring, and a touch of lip gloss. Oh! The glasses. She rummaged in her black patent evening bag and pushed them onto her nose. There! Reliability, Inc.

She frowned a little as she got out of the car, looked quickly to the left for traffic then dashed across the street. What was she doing here anyway—really? Curiosity? Curiosity killed the cat, they say, she reminded herself, pulling close the deliciously soft mohair wrap she'd borrowed from Sonia. She had on the one dress she owned that might be suitable for such hallowed surroundings, a black silk jersey that swirled about her hips and clung softly to her waist and breasts.

Clayton Truscott spotted her immediately. In fact, he'd noticed everything about her as he'd watched her cross the street and enter the hotel. The black silk flattered her creamy complexion and dark hair perfectly, the soft ivory shawl wrapped her in a cocoon of sensuous femininity and the light from the chandeliers in the foyer lit her shining hair.

His jaw tightened slightly. Even the brilliant smile she flashed as she entered was the kind of smile, he knew, that made the sleek, moneyed men nearby wish that they were a few years younger and in the doorman's shoes, for just a split second or two.

Justine looked around to get her bearings, then almost started as she recognized him leaning casually against one of the ornately carved pillars near the windows that were part of the structure of the hotel. He came toward her, his face expressionless, his eyes flicking over every detail of her appearance. Was this tall, handsome man in the superbly tailored dinner jacket the same man she'd seen in the lawyer's office?

There was no Stetson now, and the overly long black hair looked merely fashionably shaggy, the marque of a man who set his own style. But the eyes were the same— blue, and very cool. Justine shivered, instinctively. Then she remembered why she was here. She squared her shoulders.

"Mr. Truscott?" She offered him her hand, all business. "Sorry I'm a little late, I—"

"You're not late." He took her proffered hand and held it for a moment, his eyes meeting hers directly for one heart-stopping second, then he turned smoothly, tucking her arm through his, and led her through the hotel lobby. Justine caught several admiring glances from female hotel guests, obviously directed at her escort. Clayton seemed oblivious.

"Would you like a drink first? To relax?" He looked down at her, a slightly amused smile tugging at that firm, sensuous mouth. "Before we get down to discussing details?" His voice was very attractive: deep, modulated, with just a hint of a gravelly texture.

"Er, no. No, thank you. I'm not really much of a drinker. Unless, of course, you want one, that is—" She stopped. Something about the touch of this man's hand on hers, his nearness, the heat of his body beside her, was doing strange things to her composure. She sounded like a gibbering schoolgirl out on her first date with the captain of the football team. She took a deep breath. "Please. If you'd like a drink first, I don't mind."

He chuckled then, a warm, throaty unexpected sound. "Let's just go in, shall we?" And he led her into the hotel's dining room, to a secluded alcove that gave them a degree of privacy yet let them see the other occupants of the room. That's what a room like this was designed for, after all: seeing, and being seen.

Clayton seated her, then stood for a moment murmuring something to the maître d'hôtel before taking a seat opposite her.

Again Justine noticed the discreetly covetous glances of several women in the room. Clayton Truscott was either known to the crowd who frequented this hotel, or else his rugged good looks and air of authority just naturally drew appreciation wherever he went.

He leaned back, stretching his long legs under the table and regarded her intently, a faintly derisive smile on his mouth. Why did she think suddenly of salmon in a weir, once drawn through its narrow mouth, trapped, never able to find the way out again? Why did she realize only now what his slight nod in the lawyer's office this afternoon had reminded her of: the expert's acknowledgment of his winning hand in a game of chance played for the highest stakes.

His continued silence was very disconcerting. She resolved not to break it. The fact that he was behaving in this arrogant, superior manner, as though her very presence there amused him, as though everything between them had been completely settled and was well within his control, absolutely maddened her. But it was *his* idea that she meet him here; *he* was the one who had the outrageous proposal to put to her and it was up to him to make the first move.

"May I call you Justine?" he asked, breaking the silence with an unexpected question.

"I— Yes, of course." She glanced at him, then looked quickly away, afraid suddenly of the directness of his blue gaze. She looked briefly around the room, registering the faint clink of crystal and silver, the low murmur of conversation. Her nostrils flared slightly, as she struggled to control her rising temper.

Blast the man anyway! If the job wasn't so darned attractive that she didn't dare turn it down flat before finding out what was involved— If she could afford to, she'd tell him what he could do with his job here and now and leave! But that was just it: she couldn't afford to, not if she wanted to set up her own school before she was old and gray. She had to find out if she could live with his terms.

"Madame, la carte."

"Merci." The diversion was welcome and Justine took the menu from the waiter and held it up, effectively blocking the sight of the very disturbing man on the other side of the table.

"Pour moi, une salade verte, le steak au poivre, bleu, s'il vous plaît," he said quietly to the waiter, his accent impeccable. *"Et un petit plat des champignons, très petit."* The man was full of surprises.

"Et pour madame?" The waiter addressed him again.

"Madame?" He raised an eyebrow in inquiry, a mocking light in his eyes, and she determinedly gave the waiter her own order, in French as unaccented as his, her hazel eyes glittering.

"Mademoiselle!" she hissed, leaning across the table as soon as the waiter had gone. "If you don't mind!" He grinned, and reached across to take one of her hands in his, turning it over to inspect the palm intently for a moment, ignoring her weak attempt to pull it back.

"I see you are a woman of many talents, Justine. Where did you learn your excellent French?" He held her hand firmly, cradled in both of his, and Justine tried to ignore the tremor that suddenly passed down her spine.

"My mother is French."

"And your father is Irish, I presume."

"Yes."

"A very interesting combination, I should think?" He raised his brow ironically at her, his eyes gleaming with good humor. Justine nodded slightly, a little breathless. He continued to study her, stroking the ball of his thumb lightly, almost absently, across her palm. She took a deep breath and pulled her hand away from his.

"It seems we have something in common at least. My mother was French also. Perhaps our little, er, arrangement will work out very well after all—for both of us? We may even enjoy the next couple of months."

He grinned again, and she felt herself smile back. The man really had the most unexpected, potent kind of charm, she thought, especially for a man to whom everything—and everyone, obviously—had a price.

"I suppose you're assuming I'll accept your offer," she said crisply. His eyes held a brief flicker of surprise, but he smiled.

"Oh, but you will, Justine. You will." His voice was silky and warm, but all the same, she felt the cold steel underneath. Just then a sommelier appeared with a bottle of Bollinger. Justine raised her eyebrows in silent question, but Clayton only smiled. When the waiter had gone, he handed her a glass, raised his, and said, "I think we have cause for a little celebration, don't you?"

"Mission accomplished, you mean? I'm not sure if we do or not." She was suddenly very irritated at his high-handed assumption that she was going to fall in with all of his plans and with his deliberate obtuseness at her hints that she might not go along with everything he'd planned. But she bit back her angry words—for now.

"To you, Justine O'Malley, whoever you are. May all your dreams come true." He nodded solemnly, again ignoring her remark, a faint mocking smile in the blue-green depths of his eyes. He drank, his eyes holding hers over the rim of the glass.

She took a sip of the pale, cold liquid, dry bubbles pricking at her throat. "Mmm, lovely." For a moment she allowed herself to enjoy the moment, savor the taste of the excellent wine. Dreams, he'd said. She thought of her plans for MacAllister Play School, and her occasional longings for children of her own someday, and a man—

Then her eyes met his, faintly challenging. "And what might your dreams be, Mr. Truscott? What makes you think you can really get away with this—this idiotic plan you've cooked up, for instance?"

His eyes were suddenly wary. She'd touched a tenderness somewhere. He set down his glass carefully. "Finding the right candidate for the job is important, of course." He shrugged slightly. "And that takes money—what else?"

"Money!" She leaned across the table, eyes flashing. "Haven't you heard? Money can't buy everything—even you must know that."

"Of course I do." His eyes flared, and she felt the edge of his anger. Then they darkened. With what—was it regret? Pain? She couldn't tell. "But I do know what it can buy me—perhaps better than most—and I reckon it can buy me a wife for six months, long enough for me to get what I'm really after—custody of my niece and nephew."

He hesitated for a moment, regarding her intently, his blue eyes narrowed. Then he smiled and raised his glass. "And you, Justine O'Malley, are the lucky woman I'm going to marry."

Her heart lightened, stupidly, for an instant at his words, and at the look in his eye, echoing for a moment the dreams she'd had, of hearing those words one day… But not from this man! He was mocking everything she'd ever believed in or stood for.

"You're proposing to manipulate the court!"

"Come, Justine. You're not a child." His eyes raked her face, her shoulders, lingered on the swell of her breasts and she felt a warmth suddenly rise from her nape. His eyes were very cold. "You must know that appearances can be deceiving. Sometimes appearances require management." Had his eyes lingered for a moment, speculatively, on her horn-rimmed glasses? Surely not. Justine felt her cheeks flood with hot color.

He drank, setting the glass down again before meeting her bright gaze. "Simply put, my dear, the court makes the rules, I play by the rules and I intend to win by the rules. The rules say bachelors don't make good legal guardians. Therefore—I take a wife." His eyes were relentless on hers, daring her to question his logic. She decided to ignore the challenge.

"Why—why me?"

"You?" He seemed surprised at the question. "Why, because you've got excellent qualifications, of course. And you've got the very best of reasons—you desperately want the money." He smiled wryly, his glance quickly flicking over her. "And because you're a brunette."

"Brunette!" She was astonished, recalling her thoughts in the lawyer's office that day about the mysterious Mr. X preferring blondes. She nearly laughed out loud. It seems he preferred brunettes! "What's that got to do with anything?"

His eyes lingered over her glossy dark hair, brushed back simply and caught above the ear on each side with enameled combs. Justine felt the slow heat of her response to that look—detached and cool, yet strangely caressing—creep up to her cheeks.

"The children's mother was a brunette," he said enigmatically, after a long pause. He rotated his champagne glass slowly in lean, strong fingers and her eyes were drawn to the small, precise action. "She was never around much but, even so, they do miss her. Particularly Tim." His brow clouded and he seemed lost in thought for a moment. "I thought it might be—well, useful if the woman who came into their lives reminded them a little of their mother—however slightly. Who knows? Might make it easier for them." He shrugged and stared down into his glass.

Justine was taken aback. She'd never had a job offered based on such a ludicrous premise as the color of her hair, and his obvious concern for the feelings of the children was another surprise. It touched her somehow, despite all the evidence before her of a cold, hard, calculating man, a man who'd considered all the risks and covered most of them, a man who would stop at nothing to get what he wanted. And she realized, too, perhaps for the first time, how the entire plan, from beginning to end, was a carefully thought-out web of deception. Even this.

"Nanny? Another little white lie I suppose?"

"John's idea. A good one, too. He thought the candidate should be someone who was good with children and that the shortlist of candidates should think they were being offered a well-paid nanny position." He tipped his head back to drain his glass. "More?" He offered to refill her glass and she nodded. "I agreed with his assessment."

Would he satisfy her real curiosity? Without a commitment? "Look. I'm not saying I'll take the job but, can you—well, tell me what would actually be involved if I did?"

"Of course you're taking the job, Justine," he said lazily, his blue eyes narrowing in direct counterpoint to his easy drawl. "I picked you out of that lot and, dammit, I'm going to marry you. I'm not going through this again. Besides—" he paused as the waiter delivered their plates ''—no one's to know of this, uh, little arrangement, except you, me and John. You must understand that secrecy is absolutely necessary. And, frankly, I can't waste too much more time on this. It's come at a damned poor time of year—I should be back at Willow Springs helping out with the early branding.''

He finished briskly, ignoring her stunned look, and picked up his fork as though certain that he'd dealt with all her objections. ''Don't worry, I'll meet your conditions, whatever they are. Within reason.'' He sliced into his steak, *bleu,* as he'd ordered. Justine could see the red juices running onto the white plate.

''Look here—'' Her throat felt tight and she leaned forward. ''Would you get it through your head, Mr. Truscott—''

''Clayton.''

''Would you get it through your thick cowboy skull that money isn't the answer to everything, and it certainly isn't what's going to convince me to take the job!''

''That's not what you told John,'' he said levelly.

She shifted uncomfortably in her seat, and tasted the sole she'd ordered. At least her normally healthy appetite had not deserted her. He was right. She'd told the lawyer point-blank that it was the money she was interested in. ''That was before I realized you wanted to buy a wife.''

''Rent one,'' he corrected, grinning. ''You'd be free to go your own way in six months or so. After I got custody. I'm not expecting that much for my money, Justine. All you have to do is pretend to be happily married to me.''

''You're something else, you know that! You haven't listened to a word I've said. It's—it's unnatural!'' She glared at him. "You're—you're absolutely cold-blooded about the whole thing!"

"Unnatural?" He laughed, a rich deep sound that sent tremors all the way down to Justine's toes, curled tightly in her patent pumps. "I assure you I'm one hundred percent natural, Justine, and, as for cold-blooded, I promise you'd have no cause for complaint—" his voice lowered meaningfully and his eyes gleamed with amusement "—if the circumstances ever arose." She felt herself flush uncomfortably and decided to ignore his innuendo. She finished her salad in silence, chewing thoughtfully.

"And what about the children's feelings? Have you thought of that? I mean, all of a sudden you show up with a new mom, then you wave the magic wand and she disappears again—"

"Dammit! Their interests are all I *am* thinking about!" he growled suddenly, his amusement forgotten. Justine shivered. She wouldn't want to be this man's enemy. "Tim and Sylvie are my flesh and blood, my heirs. They are Lyndon's children, for God's sake. My only brother—" Justine's eyes flew to meet his, dark with pain suddenly and she glimpsed then just how deeply this man felt about the children and about the recent death of his brother. "The Mertons will get them over my dead body." She felt in her bones that he meant every word he said.

"The Mertons?" she ventured, timidly.

He pushed one hand through his shaggy black hair in a gesture of weariness and irritation. Again Justine saw the flash of pain that distorted those handsome features, and the indomitable will that drove him. "Yeah. They're Angela's parents—Angela was Lyndon's wife."

He emphasized the word contemptuously, and Justine immediately wondered at the feeling behind it.

"They want Tim and Sylvie, too. I can't go into it now, Justine. Believe me, it's too damn complicated." He threw her a look of appeal. "You'll just have to trust me on this. They are not suitable parents for Tim and Sylvie—none of the Mertons are. I won't allow them to get guardianship."

Clayton looked very hard, once again the implacable stranger she'd met that afternoon in the lawyer's office. She met his stare now, and assessed his words. She suspected there was a lot more to them than appeared on the surface. As she held his gaze without wavering, his features softened and the teasing glint reappeared in his eyes.

"Look. It's strictly a business arrangement, Justine," he said softly. "No conjugal pleasures expected—" he paused, for deliberate effect, she knew "—and none provided." She blushed furiously, acutely aware of his interested gaze on her pink cheeks.

"Well, I *am* relieved," she retorted, in as dry a tone as she could muster. He laughed.

"Dessert?"

"No, thank you. Just coffee, please." She studied him from beneath her lashes as he talked to the waiter. He really was extraordinarily attractive, the kind of super-masculine man women always noticed. It had nothing to do with personality. It was instinct, pure and simple. Just sheer animal sexual attraction, the female's need to secure the best mate—a powerful male who could offer absolute protection to her and their offspring. Survival. The imperatives of biology. Where did love fit in? At what point, she wondered, did the male need to protect what was his own transform into love and tenderness—the kind of love men and women died for?

I wonder, she mused, if I'd met this kind of man—if I'd met *this* man—in other circumstances, less preposterous... She remembered the sudden leap of her heart when she had met that piercing blue gaze in the lawyer's office for the first time, up close by the windows. And the curious tingle he'd left in her hand when he'd examined her palm earlier. Had he caught a glimpse of her fate written there?

But this idle speculation was nonsense: they were from two totally different, totally separate worlds, brought together by sheer accident of circumstance. Aghast at the direction her daydream had taken, Justine took a deep breath and straightened in her chair, to find him repeating something, that lazy, crooked smile on his face again. The same smile that tugged at her midriff in some crazy exhilarating way.

"I said—do you take cream?"

"What? Oh, yes, please."

"Penny for them?"

"I was just wondering—well, why you don't do this thing properly. I mean, you're a reasonably attractive man, piles of money obviously, healthy, probably still got all your teeth. Why don't you just marry someone and be done with it? Produce your own heirs. I'm sure you've got plenty of opportunity."

"Plenty. And, yes, I've got all my teeth, thank you. Trouble is—" he lowered his voice, and his smile faded "—I have no intention of producing my own heirs, Justine." He gave her an intent, speculative look, then leaned back in his chair. "I'm not the marrying kind of man."

"Oh?"

"Some men aren't, you know." She held his gaze. "You see, I've seen what a woman can do to a man when he makes the mistake of falling in love with her. I've no plans to be one of those men. I saw what it did to my brother." His lips twisted in a bitter smile. "Angela made his life hell—sheer hell—in the way only a woman can. The poor fool was mad about her. Blind. Putty in her hands." His eyes held that pool of pain and anger she'd glimpsed before. He continued softly, one eyebrow raised, "And all he ever was to her was an endless bank account."

"You sound awfully cynical."

"Do I?" He laughed, a short harsh sound without humor. "With good reason. But I prefer to call it simple realism, Justine. And I've never met a woman yet who's proved me wrong."

"About only wanting men for the money or the position they can provide? Why, that's ridiculous! You must travel in very strange circles," she said stiffly, feeling the need to defend her sex. "All women aren't like that. In fact, most aren't—"

"Prove it," he said, and she felt the cold steel beneath the softly issued challenge. "Make my day, Miss O'Malley."

She considered. There *was* one way to do it. She'd almost reached that conclusion anyway. The utter cynicism he'd revealed just now was the final straw; it unnerved her. This man was impossible. Altogether, it was an impossible situation—

"All right, I will." She wiped her lips delicately with her napkin, an action he followed, his eyes lingering on her mouth, then she set the cloth down carefully and met his gaze boldly, chin up. "You're right—I do need the money, but I don't think I'm desperate enough to be interested in what you're offering, Clayton Truscott. In fact, you can take your idiotic rent-a-bride proposal and you can stuff it!'' And with that she got up and walked regally from the restaurant, ignoring the mildly interested stares all around her.

As a parting line it had been effective, if not terribly original. But she hadn't got past the Wildwood Room's entrance when she felt his grip, iron hard, on her upper arm.

''Don't ever do that again,'' he said, his voice grim and deadly quiet in her ear. She tried to wrench her arm away, but his grip only tightened. This wasn't the grip of a man who kept fit on the racquetball courts, but the iron strength of a man who could wrestle a maverick steer to the ground—if he had to.

''Stop it! You're hurting me!'' He ignored her protest, wheeled her smartly at the doorway and marched her into the nearby lounge. At a darkened table in a corner, he directed her to a soft chair and flashed a signal at the bartender. Then he sat down beside her.

''Now, Justine—'' he began, very quietly. She could sense the fury beneath the surface. This man clearly was not used to being crossed. ''Just what the hell is the problem here?''

''Number one—you,'' she said, her eyes flashing. ''You're arrogant, you're unpleasant, you're planning something—if not illegal, certainly immoral—'' Justine retorted, ticking off the reasons on her fingers.

''I'm taking you for granted. Is that it?'' He raised one eyebrow mockingly. She stared at him. He'd hit the nail on the head—she resented his assumption of her automatic cooperation.

She swallowed. ''Yes.''

"Ah. So now we are getting somewhere. I had thought it might be a simple question of money and I had considered upping the ante—" he held up one hand to silence her, continuing smoothly, his voice laced with sarcasm "—but of course you're not that sort of woman. Or so you say." He was openly mocking her, throwing up her earlier words. "So, Justine O'Malley. I am a reasonable man. What would convince you to take the job? And solve the problem—for us both?"

Justine was prevented from replying by the arrival of coffee and brandy at their table. She ignored the brandy, drawing the coffee toward her and stirring in cream and sugar. What would make her take the job?

"Are you reluctant to give up your current job? No," he answered himself rhetorically, "or you would not have applied."

She sighed. "No." If only he knew—

"It's not the money?"

She shot him a venomous glance. "Of course not. The money is—more than adequate."

"Is it the thought of having to pass as my wife for a period of six months? If not in fact, in appearance?" He was enumerating the questions and her answers on the fingers of one hand, as she had done. He looked up inquiringly at her hesitation.

"No." She could do it, she knew she could. He had assured her the marriage was in name only and somehow, she knew he was a man of his word. It wasn't that, although her mind skirted very quickly over imagining the possible situations she might find herself in over the next few months.

"You could tolerate me—just?" He grinned. She nodded, smiling reluctantly.

"Is it the prospect of outmaneuvering the court?"

She considered, then answered slowly. "I'll admit I don't like that idea, and I certainly wouldn't lie for you...."

"I wouldn't ask you to. All you've got to do is marry me and pretend you're in love with me."

"Let's leave the money out of it." She met his eyes with a troubled look. "I—I think what's bothering me most, Clayton, is that I've got to feel that this is best for the children."

"You don't think I'd make a good father?" His tone was light, but this was not a teasing matter. She bit her lip, a vulnerable gesture that he noted. His eyes narrowed and he grew very still.

"I—I have no idea about that. It's just, well, it's just that I could not be a party to something like this if I thought it might make the children unhappy. Do you understand?" She looked appealingly up at him, her hazel eyes a soft golden in the dim light. He reached out unexpectedly and ran the side of his thumb gently down the curve of her cheek.

"And how, Justine O'Malley, do you expect me to prove the children are happy with me?" His voice was low and so unexpectedly shot with the undertone of pain she'd heard before that Justine's eyes filled for a few seconds and she blinked rapidly, bending to take a sip of coffee to hide her sudden emotion.

"I—I don't know. Perhaps—" it was an idea "—perhaps I could see you with them, see how they react to you—"

"But that's ridiculous! They're at Willow Springs, at my ranch—three hundred miles away. There's no time to take you up there. You've simply got to trust me on this, Justine!"

"I can't!"

"Why not?"

"I've only just met you, and you've got some pretty wild ideas—you've got to admit that." He was staring at her, his frown deepening. "Maybe they could come down here," she added in a small voice.

"Dammit!" He slammed his fist down on the arm of his chair in a sudden explosive gesture, then reached for the brandy. He glared at her untouched snifter, raised one eyebrow, then obviously decided to drop the subject. No sense dragging in a red herring, she thought, clearly seeing his mind weigh the alternatives. Satisfy the difficult Miss O'Malley? Or dump her?

"Dammit, Justine! I take back what I said earlier about this working out better than I'd expected," he growled. Then he bent toward her and looked deep into her eyes, angrily at first, then with a searching, considering look. Justine stiffened slightly, conscious of a faint warm male aura, uniquely his, enfolding her. She let her breath out slowly. How could she—how could any woman—deny this man anything?

"Okay, you win." Her eyes widened in surprise. Somehow she hadn't really expected him to capitulate. "Promise me that you'll take the job if I meet your conditions."

"If I meet the children first?"

"If you're satisfied that they will be happy with me," he said impatiently. She studied him, her head cocked to one side. Did he have a wild card up his sleeve?

"If I'm satisfied they like you and want to be with you and could be happy with you—yes. I promise." There, she'd said it.

"You're on." He glanced at his watch. "I'll meet you in Stanley Park on Sunday afternoon. Lumberman's Arch. Two o'clock." His eyes were dancing. "Drink up, partner." He gestured to the brandy and she took a tentative sip, choking as the fiery liquid scorched her throat.

He grinned at her, then, boyishly enthusiastic and—ridiculously—she felt like joining him. He bent forward and brushed her lips with his. Light as a feather and as quickly gone.

"Done! Sealed with a kiss."

She knew instinctively that it wasn't like him to change his mind and the fact that he'd agreed to her condition so easily secretly delighted her. So why, then, did she have the sudden sobering feeling that this round may have gone to Clayton Truscott after all?

Chapter Three

Saturday dawned bright and clear—a perfect May morning.

Justine was up early. Saturday was the day she caught up on all the little chores that had accumulated through the week and this week it was her turn to go for groceries. Sonia was on vacuuming and cleanup detail. Then there was the hardware and the dry cleaners and the bank to get to....

Justine frowned as she pushed the big cart down the supermarket aisle. Cat food, cat food—there it was! She pulled a box of crunchies off the shelf. The cardboard cats in the picture looked fascinated by the odd-looking reddish bits in their bowl—probably a dead certainty that Flash would turn up her aristocratic nose. Flash was a very large, very lazy, very self-centered black-and-white stray belonging to Sonia that Justine had always privately thought about as feline as a Holstein cow. She studied the picture: one of the cats on the box was black-

and-white and very svelte. Justine shrugged and dropped it into her cart. Perhaps Flash would be inspired.

Justine continued down the aisle, studying her shopping list. She'd miss Flash, actually. The big cat usually chose her bed for her afternoon naps and left short white hairs all over everything, but she'd gotten fond of her in a grudging sort of way.

Miss her! What are you thinking about, Justine O'Malley? This business with Clayton Truscott is a long way from settled. Not settled perhaps, Justine thought bending over her list and trying to put the disturbing features of Clayton Truscott from her mind—not for the first time that day—but somehow she was certain that if they were settled in his favor, events would move quickly. Clayton didn't strike her as the kind of man to waste time.

That's probably what had been in the back of her mind when she'd phoned Gwen early this morning. Gwen Porter, a single mother and friend from her early-childhood education university days, had taken over for her yesterday afternoon at the play school. Gwen was subbing for the present, but she was looking for a full-time job now that Davy was in first grade.

"Anything turn up yet, Gwen?' Justine had inquired casually. If—and it was a big "if"—she took the job with Clayton, she'd recommend Gwen for her position at Peter Rabbit. That way the play school wouldn't be too inconvenienced by her sudden departure and—just as important—the children knew Gwen.

"Not yet. But you know what it's like job hunting. And now with Davy in school, I've got to find something with similar hours. Maybe that's why I'm stuck on the play school idea." Gwen laughed. They both knew it wasn't because the pay was great.

And Justine had even gone so far as to sound out Sonia about a possible job move.

"It looks like that job you told me about is a possibility," Justine had told her later that morning. Sonia nodded, contemplatively munching a warm chocolate-chip cookie from the batch she'd just baked. There were pots and pans and bowls and spoons all over the kitchen. Justine shuddered. Her methods and Sonia's weren't compatible—thus the decision early in their relationship to take turns cleaning up on Saturdays. Working together they'd driven each other crazy. "I was wondering what you'd do if—well, if I had to move somewhere else. Wherever the job was."

She hadn't thought of that. Where would she be working? At the ranch? In Vancouver? They hadn't covered those kinds of details last night.

"Hey! No problem, Justine." Sonia waved the remains of her cookie at her. She swallowed. "To tell you the truth—" Sonia hesitated and Justine peered at her sharply. Was that a blush? On Sonia!? "Bill's—I, er—Bill and I are thinking about, well—"

"You're getting married!"

This time Sonia really did blush. She went beet red. "Yeah. We are."

"Oh, Sonia. That's wonderful!" Bill was an accountant who'd been hanging around for months, taking Sonia out once in a while, when she could spare the time from her stained-glass classes or her bluegrass music get-togethers or her t'ai chi. He'd made no secret of his matrimonial intentions. Justine had liked Bill, but thought privately that he didn't stand a chance. "Why didn't you tell me? You've probably been itching for me to get another job and move out!"

"Well—" Sonia regarded her with innocent, china-blue eyes. She bit reflectively into another cookie, considering. "No rush. I guess we would have mentioned it—eventually." Justine had grinned. Despite her scattered life-style, Sonia was completely and totally unflappable.

Justine now frowned as she loaded the week's groceries into the back seat of the Volkswagen. With Gwen set to take over her job, Bill set to move into the apartment, looked like nothing could go wrong for Clayton Truscott.

Even the weather cooperated. Sunday morning the city was blanketed with that fine gray drizzle Vancouver was famous for, but by noon the sun had emerged and by one o'clock even the pavement had begun to dry. The Stanley Park lots were jammed already but Justine managed to nose into a small space between a Jaguar and a Mercedes in the zoo parking lot.

She was early and decided to walk to Lumberman's Arch, the massive tree trunk that lay to the north of a large green that overlooked the entrance to Coal Harbour. The fallen tree was a graying memento to one of the resources the province was built on—the forests— and a meeting place for generations of Vancouverites.

As Justine approached the green, she slowed. She was wearing a bright yellow anorak over powder-blue sweats, sneakers and carrying a big Kenya bag containing sunglasses, a book, a sketchpad and a number of other useful items. Justine planned to walk around to Second Beach if the meeting with Clayton and the children didn't pan out. There was no point in wasting the entire day.

She raised her hand to her eyes, shading them, pushing the big glasses up on her nose with a twinge of annoyance. The glasses were already a nuisance. Maybe this hadn't been such a good idea after all. What would she do if she got the job; would she have to go on wearing them? Maybe she could pretend she'd got contacts suddenly.

Where was Clayton? She scanned the crowd of strolling couples and picnicking families on the green. Ah, there he was—tall and strong and straight. And as darkly handsome as she'd remembered.

For a moment Justine held her breath, annoyed at herself for the way her pulse had leapt. Nerves. She frowned. Never mind, there are other jobs out there. You've just got to find another one if this doesn't work out.

Clayton was standing to one side of the green, bending over a kite reel held up by a small boy, dark like him, and even from this distance she could see the similarities between the two. Problem remedied, Clayton stood back while the boy took the end of the string and began running with it.

"That's it, Tim. Run hard!" Justine faintly heard his encouragement to the boy. Tim ran, as fast as his legs would carry him, and, wonder of wonders, the kite lurched into the air, swayed, wobbled, then steadied and soared up. Clayton loped over to the boy and helped him let out the string, his head thrown back to watch the mad dance of the nylon kite. Tim was hopping around excitedly, almost unable to wait until the string was reeled out.

"I did it! I did it, Uncle Clay. Did you see that?" Justine watched Clayton grin and tousle the boy's head fondly before handing him the reel and walking back slowly across the grass. And that, she thought, must be Sylvie.

The little russet-haired girl was playing with a rag doll on a nearby park bench. As Justine watched, she propped the doll against the back of the bench and rummaged in a canvas bag. Justine couldn't hear her, but she could see that she was keeping up a nonstop babble to her doll. She tugged, pulled out another doll and set it beside the first. Then she clambered up and sat down beside the two. As Clayton came up to the bench, she beamed at him and patted the wood beside her. He sat down, putting his arm casually along the bench behind Sylvie. She immediately cuddled into the curve of his body and popped her thumb into her mouth. They were obviously ready to watch Tim fly his kite—all four of them.

Tears pricked Justine's eyes and blurred her vision. Suddenly she felt very bereft and very alone. The instant Sylvie had happily popped her thumb in her mouth, content to be nestled up to her uncle, Justine knew she'd seen what she'd come to see. She knew without doubt that what Clayton was doing was right: the children loved him and they belonged with him. She didn't need to see any more, but she decided to sit down under an oak nearby and observe them, unnoticed, awhile longer.

She watched, feeling a little guilty, from the shade of the tree. Where was the woman who took care of the children at the ranch—Mrs. Grant? Justine looked around. No sign of her. Her eyes came back like a magnet to the figures of Clayton and the little girl. Sylvie chatted busily and Clayton nodded, his teeth flashing in a grin from time to time. He looked relaxed and—and happy, Justine decided, with some surprise. He was a maze of contradictions! She hadn't thought that the man who'd shown the iron resolve of Friday evening, the angry determination to get his own way—with the courts and with her—would be like this with children. Children, she knew very well, were not easily deceived. There was no way Clayton could pretend an affection for them and have them respond to him so naturally, the way Sylvie had done.

Well, it looked like her reservations had been dealt with. Justine got to her feet and walked slowly toward them, her heart pounding. She took a deep breath to calm herself. Just think of the play school you can start now, she told herself. Think of what this will mean to MacAllister House. But all she could think of was being Clayton Truscott's wife, even if it was only for six months.

Justine paused at the park bench. Clayton had leaned back, stretched out his long legs and closed his eyes in the sun. She saw the faint shadow of his lashes against his tanned cheek, the high, angular cheekbones, the harsh curve of his jaw, his mouth half smiling and relaxed, lips that— Justine tore her eyes away.

"Hi," Sylvie said. "This is my big girl." She beamed up at Justine and pointed to first one doll, then the other. "And this is my baby." Justine smiled. Clayton had given no indication that he knew she was there.

"What's her name?"

"My baby?"

"Yes. What's your baby's name?"

"Sylvie."

"And is that your name, too?" The girl nodded energetically. "And what's your big girl's name?"

"Sylvie."

"Your big girl is Sylvie, too?" The girl nodded again. "So you are all named Sylvie?"

"Gets confusing sometimes," came the deep voice from the man beside her. Clayton still hadn't opened his eyes, but his smile had gotten slightly wider.

Sylvie patted the bench beside her, between her and Clayton. "Sit here. We can see Tim. See?" She pointed. "Kite flying!"

Justine hesitated, then took the space indicated on the bench. She had, it seemed, been expected.

"Nice day," she said, not quite sure how to begin. Clayton moved a little, to accommodate her on the bench.

"Mmm."

Justine was very aware of the warm length of Clayton's body stretched out beside her, relaxed, his arm behind her shoulders. He was wearing tan corduroy trousers today, suede boots and a short-sleeved cotton knit shirt. Her eyes were drawn to his hard-muscled forearm resting along the wooden arm of the park bench, silky dark hairs gleaming in the sun.

Far from feeling awkward, the prolonged silence was almost comfortable, as though this small family had expanded slightly, naturally, to allow her into its circle, just for the space of a few moments on a lazy afternoon. Abruptly, Sylvie climbed off the bench and raced over to her brother, leaving her dolls behind.

"Is it on, O'Malley?" he drawled lazily, eyes open a crack, observing the dip and sway of Tim's red kite in the blue sky.

"On?"

"The deal."

"Oh." She swallowed, trying to quell the panicky feeling that suddenly seized her. She followed his narrowed gaze. The kite twisted and turned, pulling sharply as a gust of wind caught it. But Tim held it fast, Sylvie shouting encouragement. "Er, yes. I guess it is."

Then, in the space of a breath, Clayton had shifted, and the arm she was so conscious of on the bench behind her curved around her shoulders and pulled her in hard against him and for a moment amused blue-green eyes gleamed down into widened tawny ones before he bent his head and kissed her. Her lips had involuntarily parted to gasp her protest when Clayton's mouth had covered hers. He didn't take advantage of her surprise, just deepened his kiss briefly in a lightning caress, then retreated, moving his lips over hers warmly, leisurely, expertly.

Justine's heart hammered and she felt her blood leap wildly in her veins the instant his fleetingly intimate caress had registered. Then she put her hands on his chest and pushed, and he allowed her to pull back a little, his arm still iron hard behind her. He was grinning, the mocking light she was beginning to know so well in his eyes.

"What—what was that all about?" Justine was breathing hard, her glasses askew, although the kiss had lasted only a few seconds. A few seconds of forever!

"What?" he said innocently, his eyes dancing. He reached up and plucked the glasses from her nose. She didn't even notice.

"That—kissing me like that! What makes you think you can—"

"We're getting married, aren't we?" His eyes held hers. She knew then that he'd known she was there, watching, under the tree. He knew she'd already made up her mind, before she'd even spoken to them. He'd known he'd win all along; she'd merely inconvenienced him slightly by her insistence that she meet the children. She nodded slowly and let her breath out.

"So? It's settled, then." He smiled at her and she felt her pulse tremble a little. "Kissing me is part of your job, O'Malley. Better get used to it."

"Is she going to be our auntie?" Sylvie had wandered back and the little voice at her elbow was curious.

"Yes." Clayton took Justine's hand and grinned at the little girl. He reached in his pocket and casually pulled out a jeweler's box. Without the slightest fuss, he opened it, took out a ring and slid it onto her left ring finger. Justine looked down in dismay. It was a square-cut diamond, plainly set in a wide platinum band and it gleamed like the clearest, purest mountain water. It fit perfectly. For once in her life, Justine was speechless.

"Very good, Justine," he murmured, his eyes narrowed. "Just the right amount of surprise and gratitude. You should be able to handle this job perfectly."

Her eyes flashed. His derision unnerved her. And she wasn't acting. But, of course, he was absolutely right—it was all a game. Even the kiss. She'd better figure out the rules to this game—and quickly, if she knew what was good for her. She decided not to answer.

Then she noticed her glasses, tucked casually into his shirt pocket. Confused, she reached for them....

"Not so fast!" He took the glasses out of his pocket and tossed them into the trash barrel at the end of the bench.

"What do you think you're doing—!"

His eyes were cool as he studied her dismay. "You don't need them, Justine. Why keep up the pretense?"

"But—" Her protest died in her throat as she realized that somehow he'd known. She blushed furiously, aghast that he'd caught her. "H-how did you know?"

"I noticed the day I met you that they were plain glass. Remember when I took off your glasses in John's office?" He laughed at her stricken look. "My, my Justine! For someone with such a highly developed sense of honor—taking me to task for my little deception—it's a relief to see you're not above a little intrigue yourself. Hmm?" She could barely meet his derisive gaze for embarrassment. "Not when it might get you what you want—a certain well-paid job as a nanny, for instance?"

"I—" He was right. What was so different about her ploy? Deception was deception and she obviously wasn't much good at it anyway. In a way she was relieved. At least now she wouldn't have to wear the stupid things. But why hadn't he said something at the interview?

"My vision is perfect, as a matter of fact," she said stiffly. She had decided to be completely honest, wishing she had been right from the start. "I just thought I'd look more, you know, like a nanny if I wore them to the job interview. I realize it was very silly. And I—I'm sorry." She met his eyes squarely, owning up to her error, and thought she saw his icy blue gaze soften a little.

"No need to apologize." His voice held a trace of amusement. "I don't think less of you, Justine. On the contrary, I'm impressed that you wanted the job that bad."

"But I *am* sorry. Believe it or not, I've never done anything like that before—" Somehow it was desperately important that he understand that the purchase of the horn-rimmed glasses had been just a whim, a crazy impulse. It was not something she would have ordinarily done.

"Hey, I understand. And I don't hold it against you, Justine. You thought the glasses might help you get the job in the same way that I think a wife will help me get guardianship of Tim and Sylvie," he said, very softly so only she heard. "I think that's precisely the point I made to you the other night—situations are not always what they appear to be at first glance, are they?" He got to his feet, fists jammed in his pockets. "Ready to go, Tim?"

"I wanna go, too, Unca Clay." Sylvie held up her chubby arms and Clayton swung her up onto his shoulders. She shrieked with delight, waving her arms at her brother. The dolls were forgotten. Justine picked them up, stuffed them into the canvas bag and slung it onto her shoulder. They could be just another family, out for a stroll in the park, she thought, looking around her for anything else the children might have left behind. And that's exactly what she was being paid for: to play the part of loving wife and stepmother. The stepmother part she could handle; the loving wife might be a little tricky.

Tim had wound in his kite and came up to them, eyeing her with a reserved curiosity. Clayton dropped one hand casually on her shoulder, and she inadvertently started. He frowned slightly.

"Tim? This is Justine O'Malley. I'm going to marry her and she's going to be your aunt and live with us at Willow Springs." Tim took the news gravely, his blue eyes, so like Clayton's, studying her carefully.

"How do you do, Miss O'Malley." He held out his hand. Justine resisted her sudden impulse to kneel down and hug this serious little boy, knowing that it would only embarrass him. She took his hand gravely.

"Hello, Tim. Please call me Justine," she added in a whisper. "It's friendlier. And I know we're going to be friends, aren't we?"

He withdrew his hand and stuffed it in his pocket, hugging the kite tightly under his other arm. He kicked at the grass and looked down. Justine was surprised to see his eyes filled with tears when he looked up at her again, but bravely he bit his lip and looked away.

Poor little tyke! It had only been a couple of months since he'd lost both his parents and perhaps, as Clayton had suggested, her presence on the scene now would remind him of that. No matter how neglectful Angela had been, she'd still been his mother.

"Come on, old son. Zoo's next." Clayton patted his shoulder and turned him along the path. "You know how you wanted to get a look at the polar bears." At the mention of polar bears, Tim brightened a little and set off ahead of them, following the well-marked path to the zoo.

Clayton strode after him, still frowning slightly, and Justine hurried to keep up. She glanced at him. "Tim must take after your side of the family. He's very like you, you know. In fact, you could pass as his real father—once you win the court fight—to anyone who didn't know." Her words tumbled out and she laughed a little nervously, desperate to restore some sense of the ambience of ten minutes before, before he'd kissed her and before she'd admitted her childish ploy with the spectacles.

She thought her reference to his goal of guardianship of the children would please him, so she was taken aback when she looked up to see a thunderous expression on his black brow, his jaw set and his eyes ablaze with some emotion she didn't understand. He deliberately turned away from her and was silent until they'd reached the zoo.

After they'd purchased bags of fresh hot popcorn from the old-fashioned popcorn wagon and the children were eagerly running from one exhibit to the other, from the show-off antics of the sea otters to the rather sad-looking monkeys in cages, to the polar bear grotto and back again, Clayton finally spoke to her. She knew he'd been waiting for this moment of relative privacy. But he made no reference to her earlier remark about Tim.

"I think you'd better work on your act a little, Justine," he said coldly. Surprised, her eyes flew to his.

"You can't be jumping like a scared rabbit every time I touch you like you did back there," he said. "It's a dead giveaway that we aren't what we say are—madly in love and engaged to be married."

"Look here, Clayton—" Justine's outrage was long overdue and she glared up at him, eyes flashing. The gall of the man! "This might be just business as usual to you, but I can tell you that it's not to me. I need a little time to get used to the idea. I'm not in the habit of pretending feelings I don't have, and—"

"Spare me the violated virtue act," he interrupted bluntly. "We're both adults, we both know what we're doing. You know what the job involves and how important it is that it's carried off properly—" They were moving over the little bridge, following the children who'd run across to feed popcorn to the swans. "You're working for me now, Miss O'Malley. And you might as well know I intend to get my money's worth."

She was too angry to speak. She thrust her hand into the bag and grabbed a handful of popcorn.

"Do you understand me?"

"Loud and clear!"

"Good. Next time I touch you I'd like to see a little cooperation." His eyebrow raised in arrogant inquiry infuriated her. But what could she do? This was his game, played by his rules. "Maybe even a little, er, womanly response? Think you could manage it?"

"Yes, sir!"

His deep amused chuckle did nothing for her blood pressure. They stopped, a few yards from the water and watched the swans glide up and glide away, accepting the popcorn elegantly and gracefully from the enthralled children.

"In fact, it might not hurt to practice a little. Hmm?"

Cooperation? She'd give him a few dollars' worth! As he turned to grin down at her, she stepped in front of him, and slid her arms around his waist, feeling the smooth hard muscles of his back tense under her palms. She leaned against him and lightly put her head on his broad chest, resting there for a few seconds. She felt the deep steady thud of his heart and closed her eyes briefly, willing away the odd sensation she suddenly had of coming home, of enveloping herself in this man's warmth, his scent, his strength.

"Ah..." he said, his arms coming easily around her, pulling her in tight against him. "Cooperation." She heard the rumble deep in his chest, of his voice and of his laughter. She took a deep breath and raised her face, batting her eyelashes outrageously.

"Kiss me, darling," she trilled, in her best girlish soprano.

"I thought you'd never ask—darling," he growled against her throat, placing small kisses at the juncture of throat and jaw. She shivered. Part of your job, he'd said. Better get used to it, he'd said. Not likely!

Then his lips met hers in a warm, affectionate kiss, the kind of kiss loving couples all over the park were indulging in that sunny afternoon. Justine drew back after a moment, her face flushed. His eyes narrowed.

"Was that better, my lord and master?" she asked breathlessly, not all of it an act.

"Much better." His eyes gleamed as he studied her carefully. "I take it back, Justine—what I said about your acting abilities. You're actually blushing, my dear. That's very good—very good indeed."

She glared at him, and he threw his head back and laughed, reaching out to pull her in comfortably against him again, his arm casually draped around her shoulders. This time she didn't flinch. But it took every ounce of will she had.

Two weeks from the day she'd met him, they were married.

Looking back on those two weeks, Justine couldn't sort out the jumble of excitement, the mad whirl of parties—the kinds of parties she'd never dreamed of going to in her life—the shopping trips spending Clayton's money like there was no end to it. Which there wasn't, he'd assured her with a sarcasm that reminded her of how he'd referred to his brother's marriage: the source of an endless bank account for his dissatisfied wife.

Buying half a dozen beautiful silky designer dresses at a time, because Clayton had instructed her to purchase a suitable wardrobe, hadn't been easy for her. She'd loved the clothes—what woman wouldn't?—and had indulged her senses in the delicious textures and colors, but she'd always had to watch her pennies so carefully, and it was hard to throw off the habits of a lifetime.

But that life was over—for now. She was going to be married to Clayton Truscott—society bachelor, sole head of Truscott Corporation's vast business empire since the death of his brother and wealthy rancher—and

Mrs. Clayton Truscott traveled in a whole different world than Miss Justine O'Malley, play-school teacher, had.

Her parents had been thrilled at the news of her whirlwind romance, once they'd recovered from their initial surprise. Justine had seen her mother even wipe a tear or two away with her apron when Justine had arrived with Clayton, handsome, self-assured, driving a Jaguar, for dinner on Tuesday. She realized then, with a terrible sinking feeling, just how dreadful this deception really was. In order to present a flawless front to the world, Clayton had insisted on going through the whole ritual including formally meeting her parents. Suddenly his hand, warm on her back through the thin silk of her dress, solicitous as a genuine fiancé would be, made her blood run cold and she moved away from him.

How could she have agreed to this monstrous plan? To deceive her parents, who'd obviously—she hadn't known quite how much until now—been wishing, hoping that their only daughter, very nearly over the hill at twenty-six in their eyes, would find a man someday. Perhaps give them the grandchildren they wanted. And to find such a man as Clayton Truscott! He was the Prince Charming that even they could not have dreamed up for their little girl. How could she do this to such fine, loyal, trusting people—her own parents!

It was the closest she'd come in the entire two weeks to giving the game away. But Clayton had taken one look at her pale face, her tremulous lips, her dark condemning eyes and had moved smoothly over to her, taking her elbow in a hard grip, shielding her from her parents' eyes with his body for a moment. "Don't even think it, Justine," he'd growled low in her ear. "You can't go back on me now. It's too late."

She heard the note of appeal in his deep voice, beneath the anger, and it moved her, strangely. Of course it wasn't too late, not really. But it would mean she'd be breaking their contract and would not only have lost her job at Peter Rabbit, but wouldn't have a cent to show for her part in this farce. Plus she'd owe Clayton a stiff penalty.

The contract had been a revelation. He'd thought of everything. There were penalties specified if she reneged on the contract before the six-month period. There were bonuses built in for so-called good behavior. Plus a big bonus upon satisfactory completion of the contract. It was a document predicated on the unholy premise that, for the right amount of money, anything could be spelled out and guaranteed.

She'd read it carefully, taking her time. John Stusiak had explained each clause at length. Due to the strict demand for secrecy, Justine had waived her right to have a lawyer present on her behalf—perhaps foolishly, she realized, but she really did trust John. She had instinctively liked him, despite his initial deception on Clayton's behalf, and trusted him to inform her of all the details. Except one.

"I don't see anything here spelling out my, um, physical obligations," she'd said, a faint blush rising. She knew that Clayton had swung around to stare at her from where he'd been restlessly leaning against the frame of the big windows in the lawyer's office. She'd been aware for a long time that he was anxious to get back to his ranch. The social whirl of a wealthy, eligible bachelor was something he ordinarily avoided.

"What did you have in mind, Justine?" The lawyer tapped a pen on a folder on his desk, regarding her with interest.

"I've told her, John," Clayton interrupted brusquely. "There are none, other than a few kisses and hugs in public to make sure we look like the happily married couple we're supposed to be. What's so hard about that?"

Indeed! That was just the point, Justine thought. She was disturbingly aware of how difficult it was to govern her responses to Clayton's embraces, public though they were. And she suspected that he overdid the loving fiancé act a little, knowing how it flustered her. In fact, six months with him— If he kept this up, she'd be in his bed in less than a month, and she had no delusions that Clayton would welcome the opportunity. She was sure he'd regard it as simply a pleasant diversion. As he had so often pointed out, they were both adults and...

All the better for his court case! Then, when the six months were up, he'd show her the door—legally. And she knew she could never bear the pain of that kind of easy-come, easy-go affair. This job was going to be tough enough as it was. Justine was a one-man woman; she just hadn't found the right man yet. And Clayton Truscott was certainly not that man.

"I want a clause added spelling out just what physical intimacy is permitted in this agreement," she said crisply, making up her mind. She ignored the snort of laughter from Clayton's side of the room. "I agree to public embraces for the purposes of this agreement, but I want some penalties spelled out if either party—" she glowered at Clayton "—oversteps the agreed-upon boundaries."

"That's bloody absurd!" Clayton exclaimed.

"It's not absurd! You've covered yourself pretty carefully with this document and I think it's only fair that I get some guarantees spelled out, too." She looked at the lawyer for support.

"She's got a point, Clayton," the lawyer said, leaning back and regarding his client with dancing eyes. "Come now, I'm sure she's got some idea of your reputation with the ladies—" Clayton swore violently but the lawyer went on smoothly "—and why shouldn't she have the extra protection of a clause or two written in, to underwrite her own, uh, disinclination?" He raised his eyebrows at Clayton who was scowling at them both and Justine thought he held back laughter.

"Oh, hell! Put in what you want." Clayton turned back to the window, restless again, his tall frame rocking lightly on the balls of his feet. He reminded her of a mountain lion, caged, far from its natural home. "I've informed Miss O'Malley of my opinion of marriage. Do you honestly think I'd risk blowing this whole damn business out of the water by getting tangled up in an affair with her, as well?" She might have been one of the upholstered chairs for all the attention the two men were paying her.

"Stranger things have happened, Clayton."

"I'm afraid my *fiancé* thinks rather too highly of his appeal to the opposite sex," Justine interjected acidly, with a pointed look at the man at the desk. He smiled broadly. "I understand it's a fairly common delusion among rich, handsome men." The lawyer hooted with laughter.

Clayton's arrogant summary of her susceptibility to him had settled it. Tangled up indeed! "Naturally, Clayton doesn't think it's necessary. He's made his opinion of women quite clear." She shot a glance at

Clayton, staring moodily out the window, ignoring her. "But I have an agenda, as well. I would like you to insert a clause, John, protecting me from his, er, advances." She cast another quick look at Clayton. "Just in case."

"And make sure I'm covered, too, dammit!" came the snarl from the corner. "God save me from her, as well!"

And that—signed, sealed and delivered—is how she came to be standing in this chapel, Justine thought, her heart hammering in her chest.

The muted sound of organ music faded as the minister took his position and the faintly cloying scent of roses and gardenias massed at the altar came to her distantly, as though in a dream. She heard the soft sigh and rustle and an occasional discreet cough from the assembled guests behind them. At this short notice there were only close friends and family.

It was no dream. Justine's hands were clammy and she ached to wipe them on the ivory satin of her dress. Her wedding dress, for heaven's sake! She was marrying this tall brooding man beside her, resplendent in superbly cut morning suit. This stranger! She thought of her beloved grandmother and how happy it would have made her if she'd lived to see her only granddaughter married. But not like this. This was a travesty of everything she'd ever dreamed of, ever believed in. A travesty of love.

"Dearly beloved, we are gathered here today to celebrate the joining in holy matrimony of this man and this woman...."

Justine's eyes filled with tears. She looked up instinctively. Clayton's eyes met hers, serious, remote and hard, searching hers with a flicker of some other emotion.

Concern? Regret? Could he have doubts of his own? No, not Clayton Truscott.

Like an automaton, Justine went through the familiar words of the ceremony, registering faintly that Clayton's responses, unlike hers, were firm and clear.

"What God hath joined together, let no man put asunder." The awesome words were spoken and Clayton turned, his eyes softening slightly as they met hers, and she thought she saw a gleam of satisfaction in the azure depths. He bent his head to seal their wedding vows with a kiss.

Dear God, thought Justine, her heart beating wildly in her breast as her lips met his. Dear God, what have I done?

Chapter Four

They were to spend their wedding night at the Hawthorne.

Clayton informed her that he had made all the necessary arrangements, and Justine had no choice but to
smile charmingly for the benefit of the assembled guests
at the small party following the ceremony, and to fume
inwardly. She'd known nothing of Clayton's post-
wedding plans—hadn't even thought to ask in the bustle of preparations for the wedding. Now, at least that
part was over. For better or for worse, she was Mrs.
Clayton James Truscott for the next six months.

As the band began the traditional waltz and Clayton
turned to her with a half smile, Justine felt a faint quiver
of apprehension, mixed inexplicably with intense feminine pleasure that she was the one in this man's arms, she
was the woman married to Clayton Truscott—no one
else. Justine hadn't missed the skeptical looks as she'd
been introduced to some of the high-society guests as-

sembled. Curiosity, faint scorn from some, outright envy from others; no one had expected a play-school teacher from Nowheresville to land Clayton Truscott.

"Happy, darling?" Clayton's breath was warm in her ear as he swept her around the floor of the ballroom. She leaned back, partly to look at him, partly to gain a little distance from the solid strength of the shoulder she'd been—for a moment—so tempted to lean on.

"What do you think, Clayton? Happy is for real brides," she said, with a quick glance around the room. "And no one's listening in—there's no need to 'darling' me."

He laughed. "Public is public. In public you get 'darlinged'—darling." He grinned down at her and bent to place a quick kiss on her surprised mouth. "After all, happy or not, you're everyone's fantasy of a beautiful, blushing bride right now—"

"Even yours?" she couldn't help shooting back, then bit her lip.

"Even mine," he said, his face darkening for a moment, a hint of icy scorn creeping into his deep voice. Inexplicably, Justine shivered. "Of course," he added, his eyes coolly holding hers, "I've got the advantage of knowing it for exactly what it is—a carefully planned illusion. That's an advantage most bridegrooms don't have."

Why did that remark hurt? After all, he'd made no secret of his opinion of marriage, right from the start. "And I suppose you're everyone's vision of a handsome, dashing bridegroom," she added, gasping slightly as he led her into an intricate turn, his splayed hand firm and strong on the small of her back, her dress swirling out in clouds around her. She caught sight of their reflection in a mirror at the far end of the room. It was true: they were the very image of the perfect bridal couple.

"I'd better be," he drawled, pulling her close. "That's the plan, isn't it? Steady, Justine," he said softly as she stiffened slightly in his embrace. "It's your wedding day—you might as well relax and enjoy it. Isn't this what all girls dream about?"

He was mocking her, as he so often did. "I wouldn't know about that," she said, glaring up at him. "And I'm hardly a girl."

"Ah," he said, smiling down into her eyes, a speculative look in his. "You're not, are you? I'm very glad about that." And he kissed her again, much to her dismay and to the murmured approval of onlookers. Clayton seemed to know just how his kisses affected her, and since she'd insisted on the extra clause written into their contract specifying public affection only, he'd taken advantage of every public occasion—in spades. It seemed, almost, that he was punishing her for her effrontery. Clayton Truscott was a man who was used to holding all the high cards himself.

"Methinks, sir," she said, between gritted teeth, "that you overdo the ardent husband somewhat."

"Smile, my love," he said, grinning down at her, his eyes lit with genuine amusement. "Everyone's looking. I like kissing you, Justine. Besides, it always makes you blush so charmingly." And he'd laughed out loud as hot color stained her cheeks.

That wasn't the end of it. Justine was astonished when Clayton led her to the bridal suite of the hotel. She'd thought that, once upstairs, they could safely abandon the charade. After all, there were no onlookers here. Separate bedrooms, suitably locked, would have been just fine.

The bridal suite was extremely plush—as befitted the Hawthorne, opulent with highly polished antique furniture, a small sitting area near the ornately tiled fireplace and an enormous four-poster bed with ivory lace hangings from which she immediately averted her eyes. There were bowls of roses everywhere, and a bottle of champagne stood in an ice bucket.

"My, my," she'd murmured ironically, "are you sure we're in the right room? Even champagne! That *does* seem a bit over the top, considering the circumstances. Wouldn't you agree?"

Clayton paused in the act of yanking off his formal tie. He left the ends dangling and walked over to the table with the ice bucket. "Mmm. Compliments of Helene."

Had he smiled to himself or had she imagined it? Clayton unbuttoned the top two buttons of his shirt and ran his fingers around the loosened collar with a weary grimace.

Helene de Bourcy was the proprietress of the Hawthorne. Justine had met her earlier at the wedding party and hadn't missed the hungry, possessive looks she'd thrown at Clayton under the guise of longtime friendship and bonhomie. Had they been lovers once?

"That was very thoughtful of Helene."

"Mmm. Wasn't it?"

Clayton glanced up sharply at her tone. She turned away, reluctant to face him suddenly. She met her own eyes guiltily in the mirror. Could she have felt the tiniest prick of jealousy? Preposterous thought! She was simply exhausted—physically and emotionally. It had been a grueling two weeks parading as Clayton Truscott's fiancée and she could hardly wait to drop the pretense.

Thank goodness she and Clayton were finally alone. At least he hadn't attempted to carry her over the threshold! That would have been the final idiocy in an extremely difficult day.

Justine reached up to unfasten the clips holding her headpiece in position, then paused to examine her image in the mirror critically. Her skin was flushed, her eyes bright—must have been the champagne she'd already consumed this evening. Only two glasses, but—

"I meant what I said earlier, Justine," Clayton said, an odd note in his voice. She glanced over to the side of the room where he stood watching her and met his eyes in the mirror. He was loosening his cuffs, pocketing the gold links and turning back the starched sleeves. "You are a very beautiful bride. Pity it's not the real thing," he finished dryly, his eyes hooded. "Perhaps some day—"

"Oh, you!" She wheeled and hurled the headpiece at him in a sudden explosion of fury. He caught it in a lightning-quick reaction and straightened, his attention riveted on her. She thought she caught a glimmer of surprise in his expression and felt a fleeting second's triumph. "For heaven's sake, must you go on about it?" she cried. "Isn't it enough that I've gone through this—this entire ridiculous, stupid farce for your benefit?"

"And yours." The interjection was swift and cutting.

Justine had the grace to blush. The money. "I'm not the slightest bit proud of my motives, either, if you must know," she went on fiercely. "But there's no need to keep reminding me of what a—sham all *this* is!" She grabbed the ivory silk of her billowing skirt and held it up to him, eyes shimmering with tears of exasperation.

"A sham?" His eyes narrowed slightly, then he continued silkily, "Would you rather it were the real thing?"

"Certainly not! Not with you, if that's what you think!" Justine snapped, glaring at him in the mirror. She'd raised her arms to reach the tiny buttons at the back of her dress. His eyes, dark and expressionless, rested for a moment on the swell of her breasts against the ivory satin. She flushed and dropped her arms, whirling on him.

"If you don't mind," she said through her teeth, with a pointed glance to the closed door on the far side of the room, a door that doubtless led to an en suite sitting room, "I'd like to be alone for a while."

"Certainly." He arrogantly tugged his shirt out of his trousers, unbuttoning it with one hand, a gleam of amusement in his eyes as he looked at the closed door, then back at her. "Sure you wouldn't like some help with those buttons?"

She reached up and undid a couple more of the offending buttons, then muttered an oath or two to herself as her fingers fumbled with the remaining ones. As if sensing she'd sooner spend the night in her wedding dress than ask for his help, Clayton strode forward and quickly and coolly unfastened the tiny buttons.

She stared mutely at his reflection in the mirror, her face flushed. Part of her agitation, she knew, was due to her anger, part was due to something else she didn't want to think about, something to do with the occasional slight brush of his fingers against the heated satin of her bare back, something to do with the image of him behind her, his shirt open, his eyes intent on his task. When he'd finished he stepped back immediately, giving her a faint mocking nod, then disappeared into the adjoining room.

Justine pulled her nightgown and dressing gown from her packed case, hung her wedding dress in the closet and turned the bathtub faucets on full blast in the gleaming silver-and-white bathroom. She stepped into the porcelain tub and closed her eyes for a moment as she lay back in the steamy water, willing her whirling brain to clear, to empty, to relax. But the dark, mocking features of her *husband* rose before her and she shivered. She must not let down her guard around him—she knew that with a deep instinctive sense of self-preservation. He was a very dangerous kind of man for a woman—any woman—to be around. It was going to be the longest six months of her life!

Scrubbed and shining from her hot bath, Justine felt a little calmer as she pulled on her rose-sprigged cotton nightie with the matching robe. She'd hesitated over the sheer silky negligees she'd seen in the shops, more suitable perhaps for a bride. But this was no honeymoon, and if there was any chance at all that Clayton would see her in her night wear, she wanted it to be suitably opaque. Clayton would probably die laughing if he knew. He'd probably laugh, too, if he knew that no man had ever seen her with less on. She gathered up her underthings into a bundle. If she'd had a dozen lovers, he'd never find out. It was completely, uncategorically none of his business. She turned the crystal knob of the bathroom door.

"Oh!" Justine clutched her laundry to her breast. "What—what are you doing in there!" Clayton was stretched out under the creamy sheets of the big four-poster, regarding her discomfiture with lazy amusement. His bare chest showed—tanned and broad and covered with silky dark hair above the sheets. She swallowed hard, her heart hammering. He'd startled her, that's all. "That's my bed. Get out of it at once!" What if he had nothing on under that sheet? She quickly amended herself. "No—no, don't get out!"

"Make up your mind, Justine," Clayton drawled, amusement tugging at the corners of his mouth.

"I want you out of my bed."

"*Your* bed?" He arched a dark eyebrow. "Are you referring to—" he patted the mattress beside him invitingly "—the conjugal bed, perhaps?"

"No, I'm not. Sharing a bed is not part of our deal. And you know that as well as I do." She was frozen where she stood, her eyes darting frantically around the room. Then, like a magnet, her gaze was drawn inevitably back to him. His hands were behind his shaggy dark head on the white pillow, his arms tanned and muscular, his blue-green eyes glinting at her from under lowered lashes.

"Just where had you thought I'd sleep, Justine? Hmm? The sofa's too damned short. Besides—" he grinned "—the bed seems the obvious place in the honeymoon suite."

"I—I'd thought you might sleep in there." She gestured doubtfully toward the closed door she'd seen earlier.

"In the dressing room?" He was enjoying this! Playing her like a large, sleek, slightly bored cat with a frantic mouse. And she was playing the part of frightened virginal bride to the hilt. She eyed the sofa, a love seat really. So there was no sitting room, just a dressing room. Worse luck, the love seat would have to do.

"Well, I don't care where you sleep, Clayton Truscott. But I'm not sleeping with you and that's that!" She flounced over to the bed and grabbed a pillow and the eyelet coverlet, ignoring his interested gaze. "I'll sleep on the sofa. Where you—" she shot him an angry glance

"—would offer to sleep, if you were any sort of gentleman!"

He laughed, a rich sound of amusement that made her blood boil. "Come, Justine—this is ridiculous." He raised himself on an elbow and turned to her, one eyebrow raised in inquiry. "Be sensible. I give you my word of honor your virtue is perfectly safe with me. All I'm interested in is a good night's sleep, and I'm sure that's all you want, too."

She threw him a venomous glance. Of course she was! That's precisely why she was making up the sofa. The thought of stretching out alongside him, even on the far side of that big bed, his lean warm body just an arm's length away— You're mad, Justine, absolutely mad, she thought wildly, a forbidden vision briefly illuminating her brain. He's just told you you're about as appealing to him as a light standard. She made no answer, just uttered a terse "Good night" and switched off the light.

"Well? Suit yourself. If you change your mind—" He shrugged and turned to his side, away from her, and, astonishingly, Justine heard the deep, even, quiet breathing that indicated sleep only moments later.

She punched her pillow savagely a couple of times and tried to get comfortable. It wasn't easy: her feet were crammed against the armrest, it was too soft in the middle, with a hard ridge down the center, and she had to balance carefully and not move around too much on the narrow seat. Finally, frowning, she slept.

Once, at about two o'clock, she fell off and, cursing, tried to remove the cushions to remake her bed on the floor, but they were attached.

The second time she fell off, with a crash, she admitted defeat and crept up to the four-poster, pillow in hand to slide quietly between the sheets. As further insurance, she jammed a couple of pillows between her and the sleeping Clayton Truscott—the bed was well-supplied with downy pillows—and stretched out. Ah, heavenly. In moments she was asleep, sure even then that she could feel the solid warmth of the man beside her, through any number of feather pillows.

Justine awoke late the next morning with a sense of total dislocation. Where was she? What was she doing in this strange room, sun streaming through the half-open drapes? What was she doing in this big bed? She turned her head slightly. She was alone, but she heard the sound of the shower running in the bathroom and then it all came back to her in a flood. She'd slept in the Hawthorne's bridal bed with Clayton Truscott!

Sleep, of course, was the operative word, she remembered with a rueful smile. Clayton had made it perfectly clear that her virtue was safe with him. She frowned, thinking for a moment—some half-remembered sensation nudging gently at her memory—then stretched and grinned, remembering falling off that dratted love seat. Complete misnomer for it! Then her brow clouded faintly again and she glanced beside her at the make-shift bolster, still in place. So why did she have the distinct impression that she'd spent the night cuddled up beside a big, warm body?

Justine shook her head and her lips curved again. To tell the truth, she felt great! She'd had a good night's sleep and it looked like the sun was shining. She felt ready to take on anything again—even Clayton Truscott.

"Good morning!" The object of her thoughts emerged from the bathroom, one towel draped around his bare shoulders, one arrogantly cinched around his waist. Justine automatically pulled the sheet a little

higher across her breasts and swallowed. Take on anything? Who was she kidding? Lord, he was gorgeous!

No woman could be indifferent to that kind of sheer
male beauty, she thought, as her eyes took in his long,
lean legs, his broad, tanned chest covered with dark silky
hair, tapering down over flat stomach muscles to the
white towel around his hips. Mesmerized, she watched
the shifting play of hard muscle under smooth skin as he
reached up to give his hair a brisk last rub with the towel
around his neck then tossed it casually onto a chair.
"Well, Sleeping Beauty? Did you have a good night?"
He grinned.

"Yes, thank you." She knew he was thinking of her
determination to sleep on the sofa last night and she
wasn't going to give him the satisfaction of an explanation. He continued to grin down at her, hands on hips,
hair tousled, eyes glinting with amusement at her obvious discomfiture. "Haven't you got a robe or something?"

"Robe?" He looked down at his towel with mock
astonishment. "You see more than this on the beach,
Justine. Why the prudery? You're no schoolgirl. Besides—" he winked at her as she glared "—we're married."

A knock at the door interrupted Justine's sharp reply. Clayton opened the door enough to allow a silver
trolley to be rolled in by an extremely impassive bell-
hop, then closed it again.

"Ah—excellent timing. That should eliminate any
rumors to the contrary," Clayton murmured, and shot
her a grin of sheer wicked amusement. She wrinkled her
brow. What on earth was he talking about?

"Rumors? What rumors?" Mmm, fresh coffee! Justine sniffed, and suddenly realized she was starving.

She'd reached for her robe while Clayton's back was turned and slipped her arms into it. He could walk around like a half-dressed Greek god if he wanted, but she was glad she'd opted for serviceable cotton. He hadn't missed her quick modest gesture and, with a grin, went into the dressing room, returning in a moment in a loosely belted, black silk dressing gown. He looked even sexier in that than he had with only a towel. Justine studied the trolley with sudden determined interest. On it lay fresh, hot coffee and croissants, crisp toast, thinly sliced ham and pâté, marmalade and a big bowl of fresh fruit.

"Oh, it ought to scotch any rumors that I might have arranged this marriage for reasons of convenience, for instance." She looked up at him, startled, and he smiled. "I assume that little scene witnessed by the bell captain—me wearing a towel, you looking suitably love-tossed and tousled and delectable in bed—will serve to dispel any rumors to the contrary."

He poured himself a cup of coffee, took a sip and looked down at her, his gaze traveling slowly over her exposed throat and shoulders. "Not," he went on, his jaw hardening slightly, "that I expect any rumors. I think we've played our parts very well. But one can never be too sure. Coffee?"

He casually poured out another cup and brought it to her in bed. She looked up at him, for once absolutely speechless. He was unbelievable! She automatically sat a little straighter while he lodged another pillow behind her shoulders, and held her breath until he'd moved away to draw up a chair beside the bed and push over the breakfast trolley.

"Clayton Truscott," she finally said, her eyes wide. "You are without a doubt the most cold-blooded, single-minded, suspicious, scheming man I've ever met!"

He wasn't the slightest bit put out. "Yeah." He grinned and raised his cup in a mock salute. "And don't you ever forget it, Justine O'Malley."

"Mmm," Justine said, biting into a warm pastry. She might as well drop the issue. All she had to do, after all, was follow instructions and play her part; Clayton obviously had thought of everything else, even hotel gossip.

She felt surprisingly comfortable with him this morning. Now that the wedding was over they could move on to other things—the children, the ranch, the custody battle, getting through the next six months. Obviously in private he preferred to coexist with as little friction as possible. It was only in public that he would play the role of her husband.

Husband! Her heart stopped for a moment, just as she reached for a slice of melon. She'd actually married this man! It didn't bear thinking about. She had to think of it as just a contractual business arrangement moving—so far—very smoothly and according to schedule. What was next on his agenda?

"I'd like to get up to Whistler by midafternoon," Clayton said, as though reading her mind. He raised the silver coffeepot. "More?"

She nodded and swallowed the rest of her pastry. "Whistler?" She'd hoped they would head straight for the ranch.

"Our honeymoon, Justine." He arched his black brows and reached for another croissant. "Had you forgotten?"

"Of course not. I just thought, well, we've had the wedding, spent the night here." She blushed a little, then continued, "I'd say the proprieties have been observed. Wouldn't you?"

"No." He gave her a level, cool glance. "I wouldn't." He finished spreading marmalade on the pastry. "I don't want any potential for gossip along the lines that Clayton Truscott and his bride are anything other than what they seem to be—newlyweds passionately in love with each other." He took a bite of his croissant and studied her for a moment. "That means a honeymoon. Even if it's a short one."

"Well, you give the orders," she said flippantly, curling her fingers around her coffee cup.

He gave her another of his looks of cool appraisal, then nodded. "You're right. I do." Justine flushed. Point taken! "Whistler won't be too bad. It's the off-season so I don't expect to see too many people I know. You'll only have to put up with my, er, attentions—" he shot her a highly amused glance "—when we dine out."

Whistler was a ski resort in the Coast Mountains north of Vancouver, but it had a healthy summer population, too. "I've got a lot of work to get through—to do with Lyn's part of the business. Luckily no one would dream of bothering us up there." Clayton gave her a mocking look. "Newlyweds, as you know, are presumed to be otherwise engaged."

Justine felt the blood rising to her cheeks and could have kicked herself. Why did this man unnerve her the way he always did? It was maddening!

"So I've heard," she replied brusquely, ignoring the smile tugging at his lips. "Right, then. Excuse me—boss," she said, meeting his eyes squarely. "We can leave in ten minutes." And she clambered over the pillows

she'd shoved between them last night, not seeing his look
of quiet irony, jumped off the high bed—as far away
from him as possible—and escaped into the bathroom.

Off-season or not, Whistler looked like a lot of fun—
if she ever got to see any of it, Justine thought with a
sigh as she leaned against the balcony of the Truscott
condo.

Summer flowers waved in distant alpine meadows, the
setting sun shone on the backdrop of rugged mountains, still capped with snow and even the ersatz Bavar-
ian-style village that had been created from a sleepy little
hamlet in the mid-seventies had its own particular
charm. Sleek yuppies rubbed elbows with leftover hip-
pies who'd once gone to the end of the road to get away
from it all. Now they were resigned to picking the col-
lective tourist pocket with their souvenir crafts and
health-food beaneries—albeit *fromage de chèvre* now,
not tofu—and moaning over the good old days while
sitting in the taverns in the evening. Still, there were as
many designer jeans as not, on the bar stools.

She gazed wistfully down the hill toward the village
center, where all the action seemed to be. Since they'd
arrived at the condo four days before, Justine had only
been down to the village once, and that had been just to
have dinner and then have Clayton hustle her back up
the hill. He'd ignored her, as he'd said he would, con-
centrating on his work, but instead of feeling relieved,
Justine was feeling a little piqued. Work was one thing,
but this was ridiculous! She turned, with a sigh.

"Bored?" Clayton's deep voice startled her. She
hadn't seen him in the dim interior. How long had he
been there? Now he was walking toward her, glass in
hand. As always, her pulse quickened a little at the sight

of him. It was just the situation, Justine thought, annoyed with her reaction; it was just the artificial situation they were in—not knowing what to expect from one moment to the next. "Can I get you something?"

"Yes, please. A—a glass of wine would be nice."

Clayton paused at the bar and poured her a glass of white wine. He didn't look up. "You haven't answered my question."

"Question?" She shook her head. "Sorry, I'm miles away."

"I asked you if you were bored." He held the glass out to her and she murmured her thanks, feeling a sharp sensation as his fingers brushed hers ever so lightly. "Or why the big sigh?"

He sounded almost interested, she thought, and stole a quick glance at his profile. He was frowning slightly. Justine took a sip of the cool, clear liquid. "Well, it can get a bit—a bit tiring just sitting around all day." Since they'd arrived she'd read three paperbacks, looked through all the old *National Geographic* magazines, baked two pans of brownies and stared a lot out the window.

"Honeymoon not quite measuring up?" The mocking tone was back, and suddenly Justine was resentful.

"As a matter of fact, I don't see why I have to spend every moment cooped up in this—this wretched place with you." The condo, with its three bedrooms, hot tub, spacious rooftop patio and state-of-the-art sound system and kitchen was hardly a wretched place. "It's idiotic for me to be stuck in here all the time while you work." Clayton had spent nearly every hour since they'd arrived with a desktop computer and files, punching in data, making notes, emerging just for the occasional break and a meal.

"But a genuine bride wouldn't spend her honeymoon poking around the shops and chatting up the natives all on her own, would she?" Clayton looked thoughtful, almost as if he was seriously considering it. "Wouldn't look too good, would it?"

"No." She sighed, then took another sip of her wine and moved away from him to stand at the balcony's edge again. He was right. She'd let herself forget the game they were playing—briefly. "I'm sorry. I guess I'm just not used to this inactivity. It gets on my nerves." She glanced at him, sideways. He'd come to join her and was leaning against the railing beside her. "Sorry. I don't mean to sound so sulky."

He smiled at her in the half dusk. "I know. You just can't help it. You're a woman and you are probably suffering from shopping withdrawal." She stared at him. Was he teasing her? He grinned and finished off his beer. "You know—?" he gave her an exaggerated look of inquiry "—the malaise that sets in when a woman hasn't bought anything pretty or new or shiny for a couple of days?"

She laughed; she couldn't help it. At the light, happy sound he turned to look at her intently, as though seeing her for the first time.

She was laughing up at him, openly, naturally, her eyes shining like warmest amber in the soft evening light. "I don't know where you get your ridiculous ideas of women, Clayton—it certainly can't be that you haven't known quite a few—"

"No," he murmured, interrupting her and giving her a slow smile and an appraisal that made her skin burn, "I have known one or two. Quite well." Then the smile faded slowly, and she took a hasty sip of her wine, feeling a sudden chill. "And I haven't met one yet who wasn't ready to sell her soul for a bauble of one kind of another.''

"What rubbish!" She laughed, completely disregarding his comment as something designed simply to provoke argument. Shopping! She hated it; to her it was just another of those mundane jobs that needed doing once in a while, like vacuuming the drapes, or polishing her shoes. It wasn't shopping she wanted, it was—What did she want? She held herself with both arms, consciously trying to still the tremor she suddenly felt.

Clayton set down his empty glass and put his arm around her. "Cold?" It was just a simple, friendly gesture, she knew. That's all.

"No." She looked up at him, very conscious of the warmth of his body next to hers, troubled still at her inward thoughts.

"Hungry?" He was grinning down at her, then, and Justine felt her pulse quicken a little, automatically.

"Well—I am, actually." Cooking for herself while Clayton ate in the study, or ordering out for a meal was not Justine's idea of dining pleasure, though. She sighed. "I'll go see what's in the freezer."

"Grab your jacket."

"What?" She looked up, a little startled at his unexpected tone. Clayton sounded almost pleased. He'd already picked up her jacket and now was holding it out to her, smiling broadly.

"Let's go out. I think it's time I showed the town my new bride."

Chapter Five

"*Knit three white, knit two brown, knit three white—* Oh!" The yarn was snarled hopelessly and the dratted brown strand had disappeared. What a mess! Justine jammed the crumpled pattern into the side pocket of the Jaguar and reached down into the mass of yarn at her feet, groping for the ball of brown yarn. She muttered to herself, trying to ignore Clayton's highly amused glance in the driver's seat next to her. How did the pattern company expect a beginner knitter to handle this?

"I thought you told me you could knit." Clayton's hair was ruffled in the breeze from the open window and he looked relaxed and younger than his thirty-five years as he coolly negotiated the hairpin curves of the Fraser Canyon highway. They were nearly to Spence's Bridge. On one side was the steep rocky mountainside, on the other the deep gorge of the mighty river far below. It had been mainly to keep her mind off the precipitous canyon that Justine had decided to tackle the sweater kit she'd picked out three days earlier, when she and Clayton had explored the streets of Whistler hand in hand, to all appearances the perfect honeymooning pair. Thank goodness Clayton hadn't asked her to help drive today!

"Of course I can knit!" Justine located the renegade brown ball and turned to him, her face red, her hair mussed, her eyes triumphant. "It's just that my previous efforts have been limited to straightforward items in one color, that's all."

"Like what?"

"Oh, scarves and slippers—that sort of thing." She dismissed the subject airily, winding up the yarn. No need to tell him that her most complicated effort had been the pair of slippers she'd knit in Girl Guides. That wasn't the point. She'd needed something to busy herself with. The week of enforced idleness at Whistler had nearly driven her mad.

The one evening they'd gone out together to explore had been different, though—almost fun, in the beginning. Clayton had been in an unusually relaxed mood as he'd strolled along with her, stopping to peer into lighted shop windows, telling her he'd buy her anything in the town she wanted and then pretending to be surprised when she'd dragged him into the yarn shop and agonized over her choice. He'd browsed for a while in a bookstore while Justine had replenished her supply of paperbacks, and they'd lingered quietly in the town square to watch the sun disappear behind purple clouds. Then a quick summer shower had sent them running damp and laughing into the nearest pub.

They'd shared a giant plate of nachos and a couple of burritos accompanied by the local draft beer and Justine had felt—almost—like she was beginning to get to

know the stranger she'd married. Somehow she liked this
Clayton Truscott better. The mask of irony and ruth-
lessness that he wore in the city seemed to have disappeared—at least momentarily. She'd only seen it surface
once.

They'd argued good-naturedly about the selection of
tunes Clayton was going to play on the old-fashioned
jukebox at one end of the bar, and he had just returned,
the opening strains of an Ian Tyson oldie playing in the
background, when she saw him pause at their booth, his
eyes narrowed for a few seconds as he looked across the
room, his jaw tight.

"What's the matter?" Justine had said, looking up,
sorry to see the easiness they'd shared disappear so rapidly.

"Nothing." Then he'd dropped onto the upholstered
leather bench and smoothly slid over so that he was right
beside her. It was such an unexpected move that Justine
stiffened, sitting straight up.

"C'mere, darlin'," he'd drawled softly, putting one
arm around her and pulling her toward him. Startled
hazel eyes looked searchingly into deep blue-green ones.
What was going on? But she didn't pull back. His gaze
dropped to her mouth and he traced her upper lip with
his thumb, sending a tiny shiver down her spine.

"Clayton, I—" she began, not quite sure what she
intended to say.

"This qualify as public enough for our agreement,
Mrs. Truscott?" he breathed, his mouth just inches from
hers. The pub was noisy, but she heard him perfectly.

Agreement? Public? But before she could demand an
explanation he'd moved closer and covered her mouth
with his. His lips were warm, firm, inviting. He pulled
her closer and she leaned into him, holding her breath

for a moment, incapable of resistance. Clayton groaned slightly and raised one hand to her nape, the other arm holding her tight. He twisted a little, turning her into him, so that her head was resting against his shoulder and his body came between her and any curious eyes they might attract, even though their booth was fairly private. Suddenly the kiss that had begun so deliberately and so lightly was neither deliberate nor light. His tongue traced the outline of her lips and she gasped, opening her mouth to welcome him. His kiss deepened, tasting, touching, exploring the sweetness of her mouth and Justine felt a melting sensation deep inside her, a dark hot whirling that began to blur reason as the kiss went on and on. He hadn't kissed her since their wedding reception and—

But he'd never kissed her like *this* before, this intimately, this passionately, as though he truly wanted her, as a man wants a woman. She wanted him to touch her, she realized, responding eagerly. She'd missed his kisses.

She suddenly realized that this was no longer just part of a game they were playing for the public and she knew he felt the difference, too. The tenor of his breathing changed as he finally wrenched his mouth from hers, almost angrily, drawing in a deep, ragged breath and muttering something indistinguishable. Then he kissed her again, demanding more and this time Justine was only too ready to give. She reached up, pulled him down to her, closer, her fingers buried in his thick, soft hair. She'd forgotten where they were, her skin felt hot and cold by turns and her heart was beating like a wild thing.

"My, my…isn't this sweet? The honeymooners." The amused drawl of a woman's voice cut through the soft haze of pleasure.

Justine pulled back, dazed, leaning against Clayton's shoulder, and he pulled her in tight against him in a protective, possessive gesture. Already he seemed to have recovered and was looking at the woman who'd spoken and her male companion with barely concealed distaste. He had the same grim look he'd had just before he'd sat down at their booth and Justine suddenly realized that he'd seen the woman before he'd kissed her. He had planned that kiss deliberately. He'd faked it! But the deep thud of his heart that she felt hammering beneath her cheek had not been faked, and that fact, oddly, lessened her anger. She sat a little straighter.

"Darling, I'd like you to meet Natalie Ransom—*Mrs*. Ransom—and her, uh, friend, Bruce Woods—" Clayton cocked a derisive brow at the silver-haired woman and the handsome boyish-looking man before them, then he smiled and looked down at her. "My wife—Justine." Just for one wild and crazy second Justine imagined that the warm intimate tone, the smile that promised so much, really were meant for her. *His wife...*

"So it's true then? I'd heard you'd up and got married all of a sudden," the other woman said laughingly, turning to slide one slender arm around her companion's waist, yet eyeing Clayton with what Justine could only describe as a hungry look. "And how are my darling niece and nephew? I suppose you've got them hidden away at Willow Springs—for now?"

"They're at Willow Springs," Clayton replied evenly. "It's their home, Natalie, and it's where they're going to stay. Of course you're welcome to visit them any time. They're hardly hidden away."

She laughed. "Oh, gracious! What a joker—as if the Nicola Valley wasn't the end of the road to nowhere. Nothing but cows and dusty old hills full of sagebrush.

Heaven only knows why you've stuck it out there all these years, Clayton. I got away as soon as I could and Angela certainly wouldn't stand for it.''

"Angela wouldn't stand for a lot of things," Clayton said quietly with meaning, then with an indecipherable look at Justine, he continued briskly, "Up for the skiing? I hear the spring snow is still pretty good."

"Great!" Natalie's friend nodded and flashed a dazzling white smile, Madison Avenue's perfect image of the jet-setting playboy. Beside him, Clayton's dark good looks looked almost rough-hewn. But although there probably weren't many years between them, there was no question as to which was the boy and which was the man.

"Well, if you'll excuse us—" Clayton took Justine's arm firmly. "I won't invite you to join us since we're just leaving." He'd smiled at Justine and hustled her out of the bar, nodding once again curtly to the newcomers.

So *that* was Natalie, Tim and Sylvie's aunt and the daughter of the conniving Mertons who were trying to get guardianship of the children, to regain some of the influence over the Truscott fortune that they'd lost when their other daughter, Angela, was killed. Clayton had filled her in very briefly on the situation. He suspected Natalie was the brains and energy behind the parents' application for custody.

But none of it explained why he'd kissed her and, more, why he'd kissed her like he had....

All of which had ended up in their first really violent argument when Clayton had refused to justify himself, had refused even to discuss it. Then, as she'd continued to storm at him during the long walk back up to the condo he'd finally turned on her silently and, making a mockery of checking both ways to make sure the situation was suitably public, he'd leaned her against a stone half wall lining the path and put his arms around her and kissed her again.

She tried to pull away, angry beyond words at such high-handed action, but at the same time she couldn't deny the swift flare of excitement that swept through her as he pulled her against him, as she met the demanding pressure of his lips on hers. She felt the strong, deep thud of his heart beneath her palms as she pushed frantically and was torn between her outrage and her unexpected desire to go on touching him. Finally, he allowed her to wrench herself away. She glared up at him murderously, her hair tangled, her chest heaving.

"There!" he'd growled, breathing roughly, a note of pained exasperation in his voice. "What the hell difference does it make how I kiss you? Don't get the idea that a few kisses might make a difference to our contract, Justine. In six months you're gone—" if she could have pulled one hand loose from his iron grip, she'd have slapped him "—but we're both adults and we're both human and sometimes people just—just connect, dammit." He released her and turned away, as if disgusted. With himself or with her? Then she heard him mutter an addendum. "No matter how much they try not to."

Shaken, Justine dropped the subject. She got the message—strong and clear—that Clayton Truscott was not only not used to being asked to justify his actions, he had no intention of explaining himself to her—now or ever. They had an airtight agreement that they'd both signed with their eyes wide open and it was up to her to watch out for herself in this dangerous situation. With an effort, she'd kept silent the remaining distance to the condo. Nothing would make her provoke another kiss like that.

Now, in the car, Justine gathered up her yarn again and risked a quick glance at the handsome profile of the man beside her. He seemed to have forgotten their quarrel completely. Justine was sure he had. Somehow she knew he wasn't the sort of man to nurse a grudge. After all, he'd made his point.

But she hadn't forgotten. No matter what happened over the next few months, no matter how many times he kissed her or how he kissed her, she could never forget that their marriage was just a carefully constructed legal relationship that existed on paper only. If she forgot, if she let any tender emotion creep into her own heart she had no doubt that the only one to suffer would be her. She must not let her guard down; it would only lead to disaster.

This must have been what Pandora felt like, she thought, thrusting her knitting needles viciously into the thick yarn—*knit three brown, knit one white, knit three brown*—realizing all of a sudden that if she'd only known what it was she were *really* letting out of the box, she'd never have lifted the lid. But it was too late all the same. For Pandora, and for Justine O'Malley.

It was dark when they arrived at Willow Springs, and Justine was glad. Getting out of the car after the long drive—the last mile or two over a gravelly potholed surface that, luckily, the Jaguar's suspension took in relatively good order—Justine wasn't sure where she was and didn't much care. She was just thankful their arrival was under cover of darkness and she wouldn't have to face Clayton's housekeeper or the children or any of the other staff until she'd had a good night's sleep.

But even that was too much to expect, it seemed. She groaned as she saw one light, then another, go on in the big, two-story ranch house that she could just make out under the shadows of the yard lights.

"That must be Mrs. Grant," Clayton murmured at her elbow. "She'll have been waiting all day for this." She felt rather than saw his smile behind her. It was so quiet here, with just the soft whisper of the cotton-woods somewhere in the distance and the silent blaze of the stars in the black sky. She stretched and yawned.

"We can't disappoint her, can we, my love?" he said and swept her up into his arms. Surprised, she reached up to put her arms around his neck, for balance. "That's better." He grinned and strode up the wide veranda steps. She felt like giggling.

"She'll definitely expect me to carry you across the threshold," he murmured into her ear and then she did giggle softly. "The best husbands do, I understand."

This had to be the most ridiculous entrance a couple of newlyweds had ever made—grinning and blinking stupidly in the sudden spill of light from the hall, the bride with her knitting bag still wedged under one arm.

"Oh, Clayton! And *Mrs.* Truscott! Oh, for heaven's sake—" A stout woman well past middle age stood in the hall, dabbing at her eyes with a lacy embroidered handkerchief. "I never meant to cry, believe me I didn't. This is just the *happiest* news I've heard in a— In fact I was just about to turn over and go to sleep when I thought I heard the car and— Married!" She flew at them like a bantie hen all done up in pink chenille and threw her arms around first Clayton, then Justine.

Justine hugged her, feeling the prickle of an unexpected tear or two in her own eyes. She met Clayton's grin over the little housekeeper's head and smiled tremulously. Somebody was certainly glad to see Clayton Truscott married! She patted Mrs. Grant's back awkwardly and the older woman drew back finally, mopping her red face with her crumpled handkerchief.

"Well!" she said finally, her eyes bright as a sparrow's, looking from one to the other. "I expect you're tired after your long trip and I surely won't keep you— I just *had* to meet the woman who finally changed my Claytie's mind about getting married. So sudden, too!" Justine met Clayton's amused glance with an arched brow. *Claytie?* "I can see that he's made a fine choice— he surely has. A woman knows these things." She bustled off to the foot of the stairs. "Don't worry, I'll keep the children busy in the morning, so's they won't barge in on you too soon." With a wink and a wave and a flurry of slippers and dressing gown, Mrs. Grant disappeared up the stairs.

Justine and Clayton looked at each other, both smiling. So *that* was Elsie Grant, Clayton's housekeeper and the woman who'd been in charge of Tim and Sylvie most of their young lives.

"You'll have to excuse Mrs. Grant," Clayton said with a grin, picking up their bags. "She practically raised me and my brother, too, so you can see why she takes such a, uh, proprietary interest in my life."

"Particularly when she obviously never expected to live to see you married," Justine said, following him up the stairs. She thought again what a cruel trick they were playing, misleading people like Elsie Grant, who clearly was devoted to her "Claytie."

"No. My attitude toward marriage has always been pretty straightforward," Clayton said, standing aside at the door to allow her to enter what was obviously the master bedroom. Was he expecting them to share? "I've never been interested."

Justine stood in the middle of the room, a pleasantly large, well-proportioned room with an immense brass bedstead near the big, double, bay windows. The bed was covered with a beautiful handmade quilt and the rest of the room's furnishings were well-worn but lovingly cared for, the rich patina of age glowing on the walnut dresser and wardrobe. Milk glass shades covered the light fixtures and the floor was covered in a warm rose-colored woolen carpet.

"No need to look quite so stricken, Justine," Clayton said, with an odd note in his voice and an indecipherable look at her. "We won't be sharing the bed."

"Of course we won't," she returned promptly. "I didn't think we would be." But she had, for a moment, and it was just the relief to hear him say they wouldn't be that was making her heart hammer so loudly in her own ears. Wasn't it?

He walked toward one side of the room and flung open the door to a modern, well-appointed bathroom. "We'll have to share this, I'm afraid," he said, with a mocking glance. "I hope you don't mind." Then he pushed open the other door on the same wall. "And here's where I'll sleep."

Justine walked through the door into a large sitting room, with fireplace, side chairs, a wall of books along one side and a large leather sofa.

"That makes into a bed," he said, pointing to the sofa. "Not a very comfortable one, I'm afraid, but I'll manage." He looked down at her, his expression suddenly very serious. "But no one—*no one*—is to know of our sleeping arrangements. I don't want any ranch gossip. Which means we'll have to make sure Tim and Sylvie don't make a habit of bouncing in here in the morning to wake us up, and we'll have to manage our own laundry. I don't even want Mrs. Grant in here. Do you understand?''

His tone was very hard, and Justine simply nodded. He was right. They were sensible precautions. And, as usual, he'd obviously thought of everything—even the laundry arrangements.

Later, tossing and turning alone in the big unfamiliar brass bed, Justine pondered again just what she'd got herself into. Five and a half more months to go— Would she manage? Clayton was sticking to the letter of their agreement so far, treating her as no more than a distant acquaintance when they were alone. That was what she'd specified—public affection only. Justine colored a little as she remembered the fiery kisses they'd shared at Whistler. Thank goodness she'd had the wherewithal to insert that clause in their agreement—she'd never be able to withstand a determined seduction on Clayton's part. Whenever he touched her, she knew that it wasn't him she was afraid of; it was herself. Something essential deep inside her—something she hadn't known existed before—made it next to impossible to resist him.

Justine sighed and turned over. With luck they'd manage the next few months together—civilly, quietly, at home on the ranch. She'd have plenty of time to spend alone with the children and somehow, if they kept out of the public eye, she'd manage a coolly distant husband. Maybe she'd even get that sweater knit!

Chapter Six

"Hi-ya! Get over there, now! After him, Lance!"

The yells of the cowhands, the choking swirl of dust, the creak of saddle leather and quick tattoo of horses' hooves on the hard-baked earth—it all added up to exactly what Justine had always pictured the wild West to be. Of course, she thought wryly from her perch atop the solidly built log corral, one of British Columbia's top range bull and cutting horse breeding ranches hardly qualified as the wild West.

Clayton had explained to her the workings of Willow Springs. Besides running several several thousand head of beef cattle on the huge Nicola Valley ranch, Clayton bred top-of-the-line quarter horses, the breed preferred by Western rangemen, and supplied other ranches with his prizewinning Hereford range bulls, bred right here at Willow Springs.

"There he is!" Sylvie took her thumb out of her mouth long enough to yell and wave wildly. "There's

Unca Clay!'' Justine hugged the child tighter against her and looked up. Clayton was out there? Her heart beat a little stronger as she looked for him among the swirling dust and the milling, bawling white-faced cattle, many of them with vicious-looking horns.

One thing she'd learned since she'd arrived three weeks ago—Clayton Truscott didn't mind getting his hands dirty and worked as hard as one of his cowboys each day. Or maybe that was just one of his ways of avoiding her. Whatever his reasons, she'd seen very little of him privately since they'd arrived. He was civil at mealtimes and always had time to roughhouse with the children for an hour or so each day, and he kissed her goodbye in the mornings when Mrs. Grant was around—a cool husbandly kiss that left her aching for more—but they'd barely exchanged more than a dozen private words in three weeks.

Sometimes—Justine couldn't be sure—she thought she'd seen Mrs. Grant look curiously at the two of them, but the housekeeper had never said anything. Clayton was obviously following their agreement to the letter, and his distant politeness should have made things easier. So why, then, did the knowledge that he was avoiding her hurt so much—as she had to admit in her heart that it did?

"I see him!" yelled Tim, perched beside her on the top pole of the corral. Justine looked, and sure enough, there was Clayton, hat pulled down low, blue denim shirt stained with sweat and dust, controlling his quarter horse stallion, Thunder, easily with just his knees and his left hand lightly on the reins. The horse was so well trained that Clayton barely had to indicate the steer he wanted and the horse was after it. Justine felt her heart leap as a dust cloud swirled, then settled, revealing Clayton's tall figure clearly. What was wrong with her?

"Hi-ya! Move along there!" With a final rush, the red tide of hide and hooves swept to the far side of the corral and disappeared into the next paddock through a gate one of the cowboys had swung open, then slammed shut on the last animal. A few minutes later they were quietly grazing, commotion forgotten, their less fortunate brothers kept back and driven into holding pens, ready for market.

There was a quick clatter of iron-clad hooves and Clayton pulled up beside them, the big sorrel snorting and blowing and rolling his eyes at them. Somehow, despite the grime and sweat, horse and rider both looked like they were having a heck of a good time. Clayton was grinning.

"When you going to be big enough to give us a hand out here, Tim?" he said, winking at the boy and reaching up one arm to wipe the dust from his face with his sleeve. He smiled at Sylvie, then rested his eyes lightly on Justine—finally. It had been a wary, lightning-quick glance, but somehow Justine felt like he'd looked right inside her.

"Oh, can I? Can I, Uncle Clay?" The boy was ecstatic at the thought of hazing cattle, just like the regular cowboys.

"'Fraid not, sport. Not yet," Clayton said, reaching over to ruffle the boy's dark hair, so like his own. Sylvie reached out tentatively to pat the velvety nose of the stallion and the horse submitted patiently, eyes half closed, ears flicking between the deep sound of his master's voice and the soft croonings of the little girl. "Wait until you're a little bigger. Maybe when you're eight."

The man on the horse and the boy grinned at each other, privy to some shared male bond that Justine knew she and Sylvie could never share. Again Justine marveled at Clayton's rapport with his niece and nephew, his obvious love of them. It was so unexpected in a long-time bachelor, a man who had never had children of his own and who had sworn never to have them. Just as he'd sworn never to take a wife—not a real one.

"Want a ride, sport?" Clayton touched the horse's sides lightly with his heels and the big sorrel danced closer to the fence, throwing his head up proudly, dark eyes flashing. In an instant Clayton had reached over and lifted Tim from the corral pole, positioning the boy in the saddle in front of him. Then they were off.

Justine watched the two of them, absently replying to Sylvie's excited chatter. Clayton held the stallion back to an ambling trot, his arm securely around the boy, then, at some signal from Tim, he touched his heels to the sorrel's flanks and the big horse broke into an easy canter. Tim was thrilled and Justine could see his happy grin even from this distance.

They cantered back to the fence, and Clayton said, "Next?"

Tim climbed down, his face aglow, and Clayton leaned over and held out his arms for Sylvie. Justine held up the little girl, grinning and screaming and clutching at both Justine and her uncle at the same time. She wanted to go, but she wanted to stay, too. Finally, with a laugh, Justine handed her up and Sylvie flung her chubby arms around Clayton and buried her face against his chest.

"Easy, now, baby." He grinned down at the russet-haired girl. "Don't worry—I won't let go of you." And off they'd gone, walking at first, then breaking into the easy rocking motion of a slow canter. By the time Clayton brought Sylvie back, she was giggling and laughing up at him, her fears forgotten.

"See me, Auntie 'tine?" Sylvie had never mastered Justine's name, not completely. "See how high up in the sky I am?" Justine reached up to take her. "Your turn now, Auntie 'tine."

Furious with herself for her sudden idiotic blush and mumbled excuse—especially when Clayton mockingly held out his arms to her and the children both shrilled their approval—Justine deliberately avoided Clayton's eyes.

"Come on now, you two—lunchtime," she said with a calm practicality that she didn't feel at all. She took the children's hands and started back toward the ranch house. "Mrs. Grant will be waiting and we can't be late for your very favorite lunch, can we?"

Clayton sat on his horse, motionless, watching them go.

"What's our favorite?" asked Sylvie innocently.

"*You* know—macaroni and cheese," Tim replied with a disgusted look at his sister.

"Oh, yeah!" Sylvie brightened, remembering, and skipped along at Justine's side.

Justine smiled and ruffled the hair on the children's heads.

Clayton stared a moment longer, eyes narrowed, face impassive, then wheeled his horse suddenly and galloped off to the stables.

"Oh, wouldn't that be too— Are you absolutely sure, Clayton? I'll surely be back before the Smythes' party—" Mrs. Grant's round face beamed up at her employer as she helped Tim to another ladle of gravy, her attention briefly distracted. The Smythes, neighbors of Clayton's, had invited Clayton and Justine to a party later in the month planned with the aim, Helga Smythe said, of introducing Clayton's new bride to the ranching community. Clayton had been lukewarm about the idea but she had refused to take no for an answer. "What do you say now, Timmy?"

"Thank you," came the boy's polite reply. Justine got along well with both children, and had become very fond of them in the few weeks she'd been at Willow Springs, but she still hadn't penetrated Tim's reserve. He was a quiet little boy, solemn beyond his years.

"Of course I'm sure," Clayton said. He looked up at the housekeeper and smiled. "You work far too hard around here, Mrs. G—" Justine had noticed that *no one* called Mrs. Grant by her first name "—and it's high time you had some time off. We can manage by ourselves for a few days, can't we, honey?"

He'd turned to Justine and smiled and she felt her heart skip a little. Why couldn't she get used to Clayton's version of "public affection only"? His intimate tone and his words and his warm smile had her emotions in constant turmoil, especially when she contrasted it with the remote way he behaved with her in private.

"Of course we can," Justine replied lightly, paying attention to the rhubarb pie she was cutting for the children. "The children are no trouble, and I can probably manage to cook a few meals around here, believe it or not. Not up to your standard, mind you," she finished, eyes twinkling. Mrs. Grant took a great deal of pride in her domestic skills.

"Well—" Mrs. Grant looked doubtful for a moment, then said, "Marge will be in Tuesdays and Fridays, same as usual and she'll do the laundry and dusting and vacuuming and— Oh, all right! You've talked me into it. Wait until I call Sandra...." And without further ado, she put down her napkin and disappeared into the kitchen and the next thing they heard was Mrs. Grant yelling, "Oh, Sandra—Sandra, it's me, it's Elsie—" at the top of her lungs as though to compensate for the many miles separating her from her sister, not quite trusting the telephone company to do the job properly.

Clayton looked at Justine and grinned. "You mind?"

"Not at all—I know she's been wanting to spend some time with her sister, now that her sister's husband is ill and—"

"It means we'd be alone," Clayton interrupted with a lazy drawl and a glint in his eye.

"So?" She looked at him, bewildered, a slow flush beginning to burn her cheeks. What was that supposed to mean?

"Thought you preferred having Mrs. G around, that's all," he said, still smiling.

"I don't think having a chaperone on or off the premises is going to make any difference, Clayton, if that's what you're getting at. We've still got a contract to fulfill," she said, "and I, for one, intend to keep my part of the agreement."

"What's a 'greement, Auntie 'tine?" Sylvie asked, her face a mess of rhubarb pie and ice cream. Justine wiped the little girl's face and sticky hands with a cloth, laughing at the grimace she made.

"It means something two people both decide they want to do together—" She stopped abruptly as she saw Clayton's slow grin and realized where the conversation was headed. "Or decide they *don't* want to do together—"

But Sylvie had lost interest and climbed off her chair to join her brother in the playroom. They had begun to build a giant castle out of building blocks earlier and Justine knew Tim wanted to finish it before bedtime.

Justine stood up and began to clear the table. She was very conscious that Clayton had risen, too, and had stepped around to stand behind her. Then she felt his breath ruffling her hair and first one warm kiss at the side of her neck, then another, an inch or two away. She shivered, a swift ripple of excitement—

"So Mrs. Grant is not a factor, huh?" he growled, kissing her again, a little lower, nuzzling aside the light cotton of her shirt to plant a kiss near the smooth bare skin of her shoulder. She resisted her impulse to lean against him, to lean back against his strength and turn her face up to his, to be kissed properly. Instead, she moved away, reaching across the table to pick up the empty pie plate.

"Certainly not. After all, what would we do when she's away that she doesn't think we're doing anyway?" she said archly. He laughed, a deep sound of amusement that had her smiling, too. "After all, we *are* married, aren't we?"

"You bet we are, honey. The wedding was real enough, even if we're stuck with nothing but a paper marriage now." He turned her expertly in his arms and just as Mrs. Grant came back into the dining room, he whispered, "And that's why in public I have to do a little of what I'd much rather be doing a lot of in private—" And he kissed her thoroughly, much to the intense satisfaction of the housekeeper. She beamed at them, hands in her apron pockets.

Justine submitted willingly—more than submitted if the truth were known—knowing that Mrs. Grant had become a little suspicious of their relationship lately. But the quick pleasure she found in Clayton's arms, in his kiss, dimmed as quickly as she remembered just why he was kissing her now. As he'd said, it was all a public front....

Blushing, pretending to laugh, she pushed Clayton away. He let her, his gaze lingering for a moment on her flushed cheeks, her bright eyes, her soft lips. His eyes glittered for an instant and she saw a raw hunger there that she'd never seen before. Then he dropped his arms abruptly and released her. Justine finished stacking the dishes, a little shaken by the exchange, a little frightened at the deep feeling she'd glimpsed in him and at the ready response she'd felt in herself.

Later that evening she sat before the big east-facing windows in the playroom watching the children finish their castle and frowning from time to time as she studied the pattern she was trying to knit. Suddenly she realized they were not alone and looked up. Clayton had come to the room and was leaning casually against the door frame, watching them, hands jammed into the pockets of his khaki drill trousers, shirtsleeves rolled up. How long had he been there?

At Justine's inquiring look, he came toward them and dropped comfortably onto the sofa beside her. "How's my sweater coming?" He slouched down, long legs stretched in front of him, and was looking with interest at the jumbled balls of yarn at her feet and the half-completed bodice of the patterned sweater in her hands.

She pretended to glare in exasperation, then smiled. "Not very well, I'm afraid. I think I end up ripping out as much as I knit." She held up the bulky knitting for him to see. "But I'm beginning to see the design now—see this brown bit across here? It's supposed to be an eagle or raven or something." She was very aware of the nearness of Clayton's dark head as he leaned toward her, head bent, studying the pattern she'd pointed out.

The salesperson at the knitting shop in Whistler had recommended the kit. The sweater was a variation on the coastal Indian garments known as Cowichan sweaters, heavy weatherproof sweaters in natural brown and white wool, depicting animals and birds, such as the raven, the bear and the killer whale, important to native legends. And of course, she'd told the saleslady she was knitting it as a present for her new husband—what else would a new bride do?

"Hmm. Sticking with it, aren't you, Justine? I can see you're not a quitter," he said softly, raising his head and studying her silently, appraisingly. Then he shrugged. "Well, you've still got a few months left to finish it."

She nodded, cheeks hot, and began another row, not wanting him to see the sudden pang she'd felt when he reminded her of the end of their contract. Strangely enough, for a city girl, she hadn't missed the city at all. In fact, she had almost come to feel that she was home here, relishing the quiet rhythm of ranch life and the slow wheel of one summer day into another. Sometimes she really did forget, and had to pinch herself to remember that none of this was real at all—the ranch, the children, this man who'd come into her life. All this was just a very temporary arrangement.

He sat in silence for a few moments. "I've decided to take Mrs. G into Vancouver when she goes," he said, finally. Justine turned to look up at him. "I've got to go in anyway for a few days, to tie up some loose ends with Lyndon's side of things, so I might as well take her in with me." He leaned back and stretched, then thrust his hands through his hair in a quick, weary gesture and Justine suddenly realized how strained he was looking lately.

She knew he loved the outdoor life of the ranch, and hard work didn't bother him, but she also knew he chafed at the extra responsibilities that had landed on his shoulders with his brother's death. Every evening since their arrival he'd closeted himself in his office with his computer and files and bank of telephones and modems and all the other paraphernalia that was needed to run a business empire from a distance. He rarely went to bed until long after she'd fallen asleep, and most mornings he was gone before she awoke, to begin his work on the ranch.

"You won't mind being alone for a couple of days, will you?"

She met his gaze and felt his concern, even though the question seemed deliberately offhand. "No—I'll be fine." It wasn't true, she realized with a sudden flash of painful insight. She'd miss him. The knowledge surprised and frightened her almost. Of course she wouldn't miss him! That was ridiculous....

"Good." There were a few moments of heavy silence, as though something important had been carefully left unsaid by both of them. Then Clayton broke the tension by sliding to the floor and taking Sylvie on his lap. The little girl was tired and had her teddy bear under her arm and her thumb in her mouth.

"How about pajamas and story and bed, baby? Hmm?" He kissed the little girl's cheek and smiled as she threw her arms around him, nodding her sleepy head. Then he picked her up lightly in his arms and carried her from the room, with an admonition for Tim to follow in ten minutes.

When Justine checked the children half an hour later, they were both sound asleep, covers kicked off, beds strewn with soft toys. Tim was wearing his cowboy hat, which Justine gently removed and hung at the end of his bed. Then she bent to kiss them both and close the door quietly, her eyes prickling with emotion. Already the two motherless children had found their way into her heart, and she didn't know how she could bear to leave them when the time came to go.

Imagine! Justine thought later as she got ready for bed—a man who adored his niece and nephew, a woman who'd grown to love them, the man and woman legally married and acting as the children's parents—and yet the whole family an artificial construction, timed to splinter apart as soon as legal guardianship of the children was secured. She couldn't have dreamed up a more preposterous scenario if she'd been writing for the movies!

But as she tried to get to sleep, the big June moon shining through her window, Justine's mind kept turning again and again to just that crazy scenario. There was only one ingredient missing to the story and it wasn't something she wanted to think about very much. The only thing missing was love....

Three days later, when Clayton and Mrs. Grant had left for Vancouver, the ranch house seemed very quiet and empty. Justine didn't realize how much she'd come to depend upon the bustle and energy of the little housekeeper to keep things moving in the Truscott household. The children missed her, too, and their uncle even more, but after a day or two, Justine settled into a new routine with the children and life went on smoothly.

She'd had to give up the afternoon rides on Sissy, the black mare Clayton had assigned to her. She'd come to enjoy those afternoon jaunts with or without Lance Colman, the cowhand who'd been giving her a few riding lessons while the children napped. Now, with Mrs. Grant gone, she couldn't leave the house in the afternoons, so she used the time to read, to knit steadily on the sweater or to try out a few new recipes in the gleaming, modernized ranch kitchen. Sometimes, she thought with a quick grimace, it was just like playing house—sans husband.

She missed Clayton, missed his quiet, strong presence with an intensity she didn't want to examine too closely. In fact, she didn't want to think about it at all, and when her thoughts turned in that direction, as they too often did, she deliberately filled her mind with projected plans for MacAllister House and how she would organize the playroom, and what colors she'd paint the walls, and whether she'd renovate the upstairs into an apartment with one bedroom or two for her own living quarters. Probably two—although she'd just be living on her own... until one day, perhaps, when she was lucky enough to meet a man who would love her as she would love him, with all her heart. A man with whom she would want to have children and with whom she would want to spend the rest of her life.

Which brought her full circle—to the tall, dark, broad-shouldered, lean-hipped man she'd married, the brooding man she'd sometimes caught looking at her with anything but indifferent eyes, the man whose public kisses shook her to the very center of her being and whose private indifference froze her soul.

Justine sighed and shivered as she took the last pan of peanut butter cookies out of the oven. It wasn't cold in the kitchen, not in the least. It was just— She put the cookies on a rack to cool. What she needed, she thought, her mouth hardening with sudden determination, was half an hour in the library with the old, ebony baby grand. Since Clayton and Mrs. Grant had left, she'd whiled away a few hours with the songs from the twenties and thirties she'd found in the bench, a legacy, apparently, from Clayton's grandmother. It wasn't very entertaining, and she wasn't a very good pianist, but it amused her. And while she was playing she wasn't thinking of Clayton.

Justine wiped her hands on a towel and glanced at the clock. The children would probably nap for another half hour at least....

Was that the doorbell? She frowned and glanced out the window. A dilapidated old Ford station wagon was drawn up by the fence, under the shade of a big cottonwood. Justine couldn't remember seeing that car before. It wasn't Marge Peterson's, the cleaning lady—this wasn't her day. Was it one of the ranchhands, stopping in for a purchase order or a check before driving on to Merritt?

She felt a slight tremor of anxiety. What if— But what could happen, with a dozen ranchhands easily within shouting distance? She wiped her hands again and went to the big wooden front door, just as the doorbell chimed for the second time.

"Hello?" She smiled, amused at her fancies. It wasn't anyone very intimidating at all. The elderly woman who stood on the veranda outside was looking around nervously when Justine opened the door. She was twisting the lower edge of her cardigan sweater in the fingers of one work-worn hand. Her plain gray hair was brushed tightly into a small knot stuck full of hairpins at the back

of her head and her eyes were pale and a little watery
behind steel-rimmed spectacles. She had on a faded blue
plaid dress, creased around the arms and the waist and—
a little uncongruously, Justine remembered thinking
later—a pair of very no-nonsense running shoes on her
feet.

"Er, you must be—" the woman said a little hesi-
tantly, her eyes darting once again around the well-kept
lawn and bright flower garden. Clayton's mother's
rambler was in full sweet carmine bloom against the
white-painted lattice of the veranda, a vigorous climbing rose that had been planted by her mother-in-law before her, so Mrs. G had said. Willow Springs was like
that: Justine had noticed little reminders everywhere of
the many generations of Truscotts who had gone before—hardworking, hard-living, hard-loving people who
had done their part to carve out a place for themselves
and their children in the parched and rolling hills. Now
that duty had fallen to the current generation.

"I'm Justine—Clayton's wife," Justine said, glad that
she'd caught herself before she'd said O'Malley. This
must be one of the neighbors she hadn't met yet. She
opened the door wider, inviting the visitor to relax. She
smiled and held out her hand. "Won't you come in?
You're—?"

A bony hand grasped hers in a surprisingly firm grip,
and Justine felt her heart soften a little at the woman's
shy smile.

"Pleased to meet ya—Clayton's wife, eh?" She peered
closely at Justine, then dropped her hand, her own going back to nervously plucking at her sweater again.
"Gladys Merton—I'm Tim and Sylvie's gran."

Chapter Seven

Justine's smile didn't waver. She opened the door wider.

"Do come in, Mrs. Merton! It's lovely to meet you at last. I suppose you'd like to see the children." She led the way into the living room, hesitated, then continued on. Her intuition told her that Gladys Merton would probably be more comfortable in the big ranch-house kitchen.

So this was the grandmother, the woman who was trying to prevent Clayton from getting the children! Somehow she'd expected someone a little more—well, assertive. Certainly she'd expected someone more sophisticated, with at least an air of worldliness about her—after all she'd heard of the grasping Angela and after meeting the other daughter, the sleek Natalie Ransom, at Whistler last month. This woman looked like she'd jump out of her skin if she turned around too fast and surprised her own shadow.

"Would you like a cup of tea? I'm just making one for myself anyway. It's no trouble," Justine said, putting the kettle on. She could see that Gladys Merton had even hesitated at the simple invitation to a neighborly cup of tea. She looked as though she'd spent her whole life pleasing others, and generally trying to keep out of the way. Perversely, Justine got down the best Truscott china and set out two beautiful porcelain teacups. This woman deserved a little attention. "I hope you like peanut butter cookies. They're fresh—I made them for the children." She pushed over a plateful and Gladys Merton took one with a shy grin.

"They're my favorite, too," she confessed, with a quick wink, and Justine laughed. Her visitor studied her unabashedly. Then she smiled and said with approval, "I think I'm gonna like you." And Justine laughed again.

"The children will be waking in a few minutes—they still need their afternoon naps, you know. Otherwise they'd be worn out by suppertime."

"Oh, dearie me, yes. I remember...." Gladys Merton's voice trailed off and she frowned, picking at the crumbs in her lap. "Jim'd be hoppin' mad at me if he knew I'd driven over here." For a few seconds she had a hunted look then she smiled brightly at Justine. "He thinks I've gone in to Merritt to the doc's, but I always say what Jim don't know don't hurt him."

"Why?" Jim must be the children's grandfather. "Wouldn't he want you to visit?"

"Oh, he's terrible set on this business of gettin' the kids, you know. Him and Natalie and the boys got the notion—" she went on, then stopped again. "I'm not much for it—'course, nobody asks me. Oh, I love the little darlin's and I miss 'em something awful, but I've raised my own—seven of 'em—and when push comes right down to shove I'm not so sure I done such a good job of it—'' Her watery blue eyes twinkled a little over the rim of her teacup, then she sighed. "Oh, time'll tell, time'll tell, they say, and p'raps things'll turn out for the best in the end.

"Tim and Sylvie are the only grandkids out of the whole bunch and that ain't making good work of it, I wouldn't say, not with seven of 'em. There's Tom and Willie—they live in Kamloops and got some fancy job selling cars and their wives both work—no time for kids. They're pretty set on Jim and me gettin' Tim and Sylvie. And there's Natalie—she's named for her great-granny, one of them Rooskies from down Grand Forks way, on Jim's side—she'll never have time for children not with all her sailin' and skiin' and partyin' and I don't know what-all, half of which poor Philip don't know about—''

Justine cleared her throat quietly. So Natalie had a wealthy husband somewhere in the background—no wonder Clayton had been so openly contemptuous of her and her "friend" at Whistler. She was gradually getting a clearer picture of the Merton clan.

"And there's Boyd—there might be a chance there, yet," Justine's visitor said, musing aloud, considering, her eyes narrowed in speculation. "Gloria don't work, but they've only been married just over a year. That was plenty of time in my day, mind ye!" Gladys Merton energetically helped herself to another cookie and let Justine pour her another cup of tea. "That leaves Jesse, y'know, but he don't show no sign of interest in women yet. Still stays pretty close to home and helpin' out Jim, for all he's near thirty years old. And there's—*was* my Angie—''

Mrs. Merton stared into her cup for a moment and then hurriedly dabbed at her eyes with the napkin Justine had given her. "Poor Angie, such a pretty snip of a thing," she went on in a quiet, broken little tone. "The young fellas was awful stuck on her, always was. But she was terrible mixed-up, even as a girl." Mrs. Merton sighed. "I don't say she always done the right thing, but, still, I miss her something awful—

"And she give me 'n' Jim two fine young grandkids. There ain't nobody can take that away from her—even if she wasn't cut out right for motherin'. Least she knowed it—some don't." And Gladys Merton wiped at her eyes again, fished a crumpled tissue from the sleeve of her dress, blew her nose loudly and tucked the tissue away again. Then she looked up at Justine and gave her a wobbly smile.

"I don't s'pose you're all that interested in my goin' on so much. New bride and all!" She smiled suddenly, seeming to relish the new topic, and winked broadly at Justine. "And you done all right by Clayton Truscott, yessiree! Clayton's the best one, too—didn't I always tell Angela that? He's got a good head and a true heart and he knows what's right. Always did. It plumb drove Angie crazy that he didn't have the time of day for her—the only one around here who never did, even when they were kids together. Lyndon made up for it, though. He loved my little girl, truly, truly, truly he did...." Mrs. Merton sighed again, remembering, then started violently at a small movement at the door. "Oh!" She brightened and leaned forward in her chair.

"Is that my little punkin' hidin' back there? It is!" She held out her thin arms and Sylvie sidled around the door frame into the kitchen, dragging her blanket behind her, thumb in her mouth. She looked up at her grandmother and smiled shyly, but it was into Justine's lap that she climbed. Justine smoothed the tousled red-gold curls from the sleep-damp forehead, strangely moved that the little girl should show her trust like that, so simply, so innocently.

"She'll come to you in a minute," she whispered to her visitor, afraid the older woman might have had her feelings hurt. "She's just a little sleepy still."

"Oh, I know. Don't I know...." She reached over and rubbed Sylvie's cheek lightly and tenderly with a gnarled knuckle, a grandmother's love shining in her pale old eyes.

But it was a different story entirely with Tim. With an exuberant yell, he threw himself into his grandmother's arms as soon as he came into the kitchen and saw who their visitor was. Justine was taken aback. Was this the shy, reserved boy that she knew?

"Not so fast, young man! Your granny ain't as young as she once was." Mrs. Merton wrapped her skinny arms around her grandson and positively beamed. Tim grinned back.

"I thought you weren't ever coming to see us again, Gran," said the boy, then, his lower lip a little trembly.

"Oh, 'course I was! What'd you think? Think your gran's magic? Think she'd just disappear—poof! Like that?"

"Like Mom always did—" Tim answered, his voice barely above a whisper, his eyes luminous. His grandmother hugged him tight, blinking back tears.

"Ah, darlin'. Your mom ain't comin' back this time, you know that. But now you've got a new mom—" She looked at Justine, trying to put a bright face on her own sorrow. "Look—your Uncle Clay's married and brought you a new auntie! And she'll be just like a mom to you, Timmy. I know she will."

Justine's own eyes filled, torn with grief for the young boy and his grandmother and yet she knew she shouldn't really be able to look either of them in the face: her own role here was more heinous than the neglectful Angela's had ever been. She shifted Sylvie to one hip and went to the fridge to pour glasses of juice for the children. Tim's quiet sobs in the background as he wept in his grandmother's arms were what he needed, she knew, to relieve some of the deep feeling he kept locked up inside of him. Still, knowing that didn't make it any easier to bear....

Finally, Tim looked up, scrubbing at his wet face with his sleeve and sniffing loudly a couple of times. Justine pushed over the plate of cookies, and Tim smiled shakily at her as he took one.

"Thank you," he whispered. Justine smiled back and nodded, her heart too full for words. What had happened? And when? When had the soft, silent little feet of these children stolen into her heart?

Gladys Merton stayed on a half hour longer after the children had awoken, entertaining Sylvie with a long, involved story about a raccoon that had lost its tail. Justine was sure she was making it up as she went along, judging by the series of disconnected adventures the raccoon embarked on, all apparently connected to the kinds of questions with which the children interrupted her. Then, with infinite patience, she helped Tim put together a new dinosaur jigsaw puzzle.

Justine watched the three of them comfortably sitting on the kitchen floor in a patch of sunlight, dappled with the movement of the gentle green arms of the cottonwood waving outside the window.

Really—Gladys Merton was as much a child as they were! Did Clayton know? He'd painted such a horrifying picture of Angela's scheming relatives who were intent on gaining influence over the children so that they could continue their access to the Truscott fortune, access they'd come to enjoy and depend on when Angela was alive. Clayton had not been too forthcoming with all the details, but she'd gathered that Lyndon had given his wife carte blanche and that a great deal of Truscott money had been siphoned off to various ne'er-do-well relatives.

Now, even though Clayton was sole trustee of his brother's estate and had complete legal control, Justine knew he feared the Mertons would use his affection for his niece and nephew—his own heirs, in fact—to apply pressure if they became guardians. But the more she came to know Clayton, the more she realized that the financial finagling was the least of his concerns. He loved the children—it was as simple as that—and he wanted to raise them here where he and Lyndon had been raised, at Willow Springs, in the Truscott ancestral home. It was, she knew, where Clayton thought they belonged.

She'd bring the subject up again with him when he returned. The children's rapport with their grandmother seemed relatively good, and she had to make him understand how important it was that the children's relationship with their grandparents not be severed, legal battle or no legal battle, not with the abandonments they'd already known in their short lives. He'd probably tell her to mind her own business, but she'd bring it up just the same.

She looked at the kitchen calendar. Five days—it seemed like forever since she'd said goodbye to him and

Mrs. Grant, forever since he'd kissed her, coolly, dispassionately, and left her, arms wrapped tightly around herself, watching as he strode away from the house. When had he said he'd return? In another day or two? She couldn't remember now, except that he'd been uncharacteristically vague.

That night, Justine found herself in a private hell neither her medical training nor her wide experience with young children had prepared her for: the death-threatening illness of a child she loved.

John Stusiak had told her that Tim suffered from occasional bouts of asthma and Clayton had filled her in on the situation. She'd met the Truscott family doctor in Merritt soon after her arrival and he'd reminded her that Tim's condition was serious enough to warrant her being prepared, living as they did many miles from the nearest hospital. So Justine had gathered an arsenal of the drugs and preparations she might need if Tim suffered an attack—just in case. During her nursing career she'd seen her share of tiny patients struggling to desperately seize the precious breath that eluded them—the wheezing, the coughing, the convulsions, the pleading in their eyes for someone—anyone!—to help them. She'd seen enough to know an asthma attack when she saw one.

That night, when Justine put the children to bed, Tim had clung to her for a moment, his thin little arms tight around her neck as she bent to kiss him good-night.

"When's Uncle Clay coming back?" he whispered, his blue eyes worried.

Justine straightened his covers, then sat back down beside him, taking his hand in hers. "He'll be back in a day or two, Tim. Very soon." She smiled to reassure him, then went on, "How did you like your visit today with your gran?"

"Good," he said solemnly, then his bottom lip trembled a little. "Are me and Sylvie going to go live with them now?"

Justine hesitated. Tim was obviously upset about the strained relationships between the adults in his life—his uncle and his grandparents. Children picked up more of what was going on around them than adults ever knew. She couldn't lie to the child. The possibility existed, faint as Clayton seemed to think it was. "I don't think so, Tim. What do you think? Would you like to live with your grandma and grandpa?"

Tim shook his head. "I like Gran and Grandpa Jim, but—" His eyes searched hers. Justine could see the fear mirrored there, the pain of a little boy who'd known too many rejections already. "But they're kinda old and, well—" His voice dropped to a whisper again and Justine had to bend to hear his last words. "I—I just like you and Uncle Clay better. I want to stay here and live with you."

"I'm sure you will be staying here, Tim. Uncle Clay wants you to stay at Willow Springs very much." She tucked him in firmly and bent to kiss him again. Sylvie was already asleep in her bed. She felt pretty safe in promising that much; Clayton had said the Mertons would get him over his dead body and by now Justine knew that that meant Clayton intended to have his way in the end. One way or another. Wasn't her presence here proof of that? "Go to sleep now, darling. You've had a busy day."

Justine had been in bed perhaps an hour or two—she didn't know how long. She only knew that she'd been

restless and was having a difficult time falling asleep. The
old house seemed to creak and groan in the wind and the
soft slap of cottonwood leaves against wooden eaves
somewhere, a sound she'd never noticed before, seemed
very loud and very irritating in the stillness.

If only Clayton were here, she thought grumpily,
turning over yet again, trying to get comfortable. She'd
never felt this nervous, this on edge, with him sleeping
in the next room. Or if she had, she corrected herself
with a grimace, it had been a different sort of nervous-
ness altogether.

His presence filled her mind, then, and she was suddenly seized with an intense longing. She wanted him
with a strength of feeling that frightened her. She wanted
him near her, she wanted to look at him, to touch him.
She wanted him to touch her.... Justine deliberately tried
to flood her mind with other thoughts—with her play-
school plans, with the details of her activities tomorrow
with the children, with a projected letter she owed her
parents—anything to stop her thinking about the man
she'd married. A true heart . . . that's what Gladys Merton had said he had.

That's when she heard the first convulsive gasp, a
sound that struck terror into her heart. Without even
stopping to pull on her robe, she flew down the hall to
Tim and Sylvie's room.

Tim was half sitting in bed, his face white, his eyes
huge. "I can't breathe—" he gasped, his pupils dilated
with fear.

"There, there, try and relax, Tim." She felt his forehead; it was damp with perspiration and unnaturally
cool. He seized her hand and clutched at it, and for a
moment he seemed to be breathing a little more easily,

his breath coming in shallow, raspy wheezes. Justine raced to the bathroom to wring out a facecloth.

"Shh, I'm here now, darling," she soothed, wiping the sweat from his face, her mind racing with details. What had Dr. Crisp said? That unlike some asthma sufferers, whose attacks were related to various allergens like pollen or dust, Tim's asthma attacks seemed stress related. Although they were something the doctors expected to lessen as he grew older, as his life settled down and stabilized, the attacks were nonetheless very real, and a serious asthma attack could be life-threatening.

Had it been his grandmother's visit? Had he been upset over the possibility of leaving Willow Springs? Or was it that his grandmother must have been a reminder of his mother and her recent death? Was he afraid of Grandpa Jim, as it had seemed at one point?

Justine wiped the boy's face and arms again, then gently rubbed his chest.

"Will you be all right for a minute, Tim? I want to get your medicine—" But Tim's eyes flared with fear and he clutched at her arm again.

"Don't leave me. Don't leave me. Please!" And he was overcome with a coughing spasm that racked his thin body. Justine held him, her heart racing with fear. Where was Clayton? She needed him! Why had he picked this time of all times to leave the ranch?

But Clayton wasn't here, and she'd have to deal with this herself.

Tim sank back to the pillow, exhausted from his coughing fit, and his eyes closed. He was breathing again, albeit very shallowly and with a labored rasp that Justine knew did not bode well. She went to the locked cupboard at one side of the room and stretched up, reaching for the oxygen mask that was kept there, and the portable oxygen cylinder.

Quickly, smoothly, her fingers working with the ease of practice, Justine measured out the medication that would help dilate Tim's breathing passages. She poured it into the special cup on the mask and positioned the mask securely, elastic strap behind Tim's sweat-soaked hair. At the sound of the oxygen seeping into the mask, the slow hiss aiding Tim's struggle to get enough breath to fill his small lungs, Justine relaxed a little. Surely now Tim would get some relief, perhaps some rest, long enough at least for her to telephone Dr. Crisp and get his instructions.

It was after one in the morning when she called and she had to get the doctor out of bed.

"I think you're right, Mrs. Truscott—the boy shouldn't be moved. Not at this stage. It's a long way to the hospital and I'm confident you can handle the situation out there," the doctor said. His matter-of-fact tones over the phone lines eased Justine's fears a little. She shivered in the loose man's shirt she was wearing for a nightgown. If anything happened to Tim.... For a moment Justine closed her eyes and sagged against the kitchen counter. Oh, if only Clayton were here! And Mrs. Grant.

"Clayton's not home? Well, somebody should stay with Tim and keep an eye on him. I'll be at my office in the morning, but if he worsens, don't hesitate to call again and I'll come out to the ranch," Dr. Crisp was saying. "I think you'll find that bronchodilator I gave you works pretty well—you'll know when to use it...." Justine listened to the rest of his instructions, nodding. She hung up the phone, then stopped for a few seconds, head to one side.

Was that a child's cry? She raced back up the stairs. If Tim had the breath to cry, that was a very good sign.

But it wasn't Tim. He was still resting quietly, eyes closed, his breathing raspy and shallow. Sylvie was sitting up in her bed, rubbing her eyes and whimpering.

"Oh, sweetheart! Did we wake you up with the light on?" She cuddled the child's warm body against her own. Sylvie nodded sleepily, still clutching her favorite blanket. "How would you like to sleep in my big bed for the rest of the night? And you can take Teddy with you."

The little girl nodded again and nestled down on Justine's shoulder, almost asleep again. Justine gathered up Sylvie's precious battered stuffed bear and carried the little girl down the hall to her room, tucking her in snugly under the quilt and bending to kiss her softly on the cheek. She tiptoed out, leaving the door ajar, unwilling just then to deal with the feelings the little girl had aroused in her.

Tim was restless again and making choked little sounds of distress. Justine felt his forehead and checked his vital signs. So far, so good. A warm sponge bath, though, would probably help him relax. Maybe then the attack would pass and Tim would be able to get some of the sleep he so desperately needed.

She undressed him and sponged his tanned, sturdy limbs with warm water, talking to him quietly and smiling to herself as she looked at his skinned knees and eternally grimy fingernails. He might suffer from the occasional asthma attack, but he was not a sickly child. His blue eyes looked up trustingly into hers and she suddenly had a flash of what Clayton's children would look like—dark like their father, with those startling Truscott eyes, eyes that saw right through a person, eyes that probed through the carefully clad exterior of a per-

son and looked right into the soul. Clayton's babies—
The thought stabbed at her painfully and she bent to kiss
Tim lightly.

This is a job, Justine O'Malley, she reminded herself
deliberately, taking a deep breath. Remember, it's just a
job. But it was no use—this had stopped being a job for
her weeks ago, if it ever really had been.

Justine gently toweled Tim dry and helped him into
clean pajamas. She quickly remade his rumpled bed and
settled him in, lowering the oxygen tent around him.
Hair brushed and face shiny, he looked almost normal
again. But his breathing was still very congested and his
eyes looked haunted. Perhaps she should give him the
injection that Dr. Crisp had recommended, medicine
that would let him relax and sleep.

She got out her medical supplies and noticed that her
hand was shaking slightly as she drew exactly the right
amount of the colorless drug into the syringe. It was idiotic—she'd done this hundreds of times before! But
never to a child she loved, she realized, as she gave Tim
the injection, wincing as he winced at the pinprick of
pain, feeling it as he did, sorry that she'd had to cause
him even the slightest amount of pain for the best of
reasons.

Finally, Tim slept, his breathing gradually calming
and becoming more relaxed. Justine glanced at her
watch. Almost half past two! She sat down in the big
upholstered chair beside Tim's bed, the chair Clayton sat
in to read the children their bedtime stories, and pulled
her legs up under her. The cotton nightshirt rode up, ex-
posing her bare thighs and she shivered a little again. It
wasn't cold in the children's room but she'd got a little
damp from giving Tim the sponge bath and— Justine
yawned and put her head back on the chair. She'd just

rest here, just a few more minutes, then check on Tim again. She opened her eyes slowly. Perhaps she'd stretch out on Sylvie's bed for the rest of the night....

Then she closed her eyes again. This was heaven. Just to rest, to relax, to dream perhaps.... How had it happened, she mused sleepily to herself. When had she fallen in love with the children, after all? And when, came the thought fast on its heels, a thought she didn't even pause to examine, when had she fallen in love with their uncle—her own husband? As she knew without a single doubt she had, in that warm, half-swimming place of truth between sleep and waking, between head and heart.

What had awakened her? Had she heard the far-off sound of a door opening and closing? Had the slap-slap of the cottonwoods outside the darkened window finally penetrated her dreams? Had Tim moved uneasily in his sleep and disturbed her, tuned as she was to the boy breathing freely and easily, asleep beside her?

Or had she felt a slight change in the very texture of the air that told her of a presence once again in the old house, a presence that belonged here with them and for which they had all waited?

When she awoke, he was there. That was all that she knew.

He was standing at the open door to Tim's room, his face strained and tired, his eyes shadowed with fear for the boy as he quickly took in the situation—the oxygen mask, the medical bag, the slim young woman curled up in the big chair, her dark hair awry, her arms folded on her bare knees. The woman he'd—

She closed her eyes. She must be dreaming—she had conjured up his presence somehow out of her great longing. She opened her eyes again. He was still there. She moistened dry lips with her tongue.

"Clayton?" she whispered.

"Is he—?" His voice was harsh with concern.

"He—he's all right," she answered, her voice barely above a whisper. She closed her eyes again, resting, testing her reaction to his presence here. "He's all right now."

"Thank God!" She opened her eyes again and this time their gaze met across the room, steadied, locked. The room became very still around her. Tears pricked her eyes. He was really here... he had come back!

"Oh, Clayton...." He took a step toward her, his eyes intent, and with a soft, broken cry she flew into his arms.

Chapter Eight

Clayton's arms closed around her strong and tight.

"Oh, my darling Justine," he said, over and over again, his voice thick with weariness and emotion. "Don't cry, my sweet darling—please don't cry."

But she did; she cried buckets. Clinging to him, burying her face in his shirt, she wept, trying at the same time to tell him about Tim, about Gladys Merton, about how scared she'd been and how she'd needed him there tonight and how glad she was that he'd come.... She wanted to tell him that she loved him and that she'd missed him terribly and that she was sorry, so sorry, for the hideous mess she'd got herself into, after all his warnings—but, of course, she didn't dare.

They stood there for a long time, his dark head bent over hers, gently pushing back strands of hair from her damp face with his lips, the shadow of stubble on his jaw and chin feeling slightly scratchy, and pleasant. He kissed her softly on her forehead, her cheek, the shining crown of her head.

Gradually her sobs quieted, and she became aware of the length of her body warm against his, of him holding her close, kneading the tense muscles of her back and smoothing her flesh from shoulder to hip through the thin fabric of her nightshirt with long, firm strokes of his hands. She became aware of just how little she had on and how short her nightshirt was, just brushing the tops of her thighs as she leaned against him, weak with exhaustion—and with something else. Something warm, something that grew stronger inside her, a faint flutter within that made her look up at him finally, her eyelashes spiky with tears.

He had never looked so serious, she remembered thinking later. He had never looked at her so solemnly nor with such intentness. She watched him as he looked slowly at her eyes, her cheeks shiny with tears, her mouth, still trembling. Then he looked deep into her eyes again, forever and ever it seemed, and bent his head to hers. He brushed her lips lightly with his, breathing deeply, and she felt a slight tremor shudder through him, beneath her palms flat on his back, her arms tight around him.

She raised her face to his, pushing up on tiptoe slightly to meet him, faintly troubled at his reserve. There could be nothing—nothing—between them now. She needed him, his touch, as he needed her. She could sense his need, knew it, felt it as though it were her own.

"Oh, Clayton—" she breathed against his mouth "—I missed you so—"

"Justine!" And with that short exclamation of her name he lowered his mouth against hers, moving this way then that way to match their mouths perfectly, pulling her body tight against him, moving against her slightly until all the feminine softnesses of her body fit perfectly with the hard male planes of his.

She gasped and arched against him, giving him access to the dark sweetness of her mouth, reveling in the taste of him, the scent of him, the strength of his body pressed against hers. They were perfect together; she'd known they would be.

He kissed her hungrily, like a man half-starved, greedy for her touch, her kisses, the softness of her body. He moved and felt the white-hot knife of desire as she arched against him, her innocent and unrestrained response nearly snapping his control. He kissed her as he'd wanted to kiss her for weeks, touching and loosing the passion that he'd known was in her, a desperate need that he knew was as new and startling and fierce for her as it was for him.

He'd wanted her in his arms like this since the first day he'd met her, when she'd snarled at him across the table at the Hawthorne, when she'd stomped out on him with her chin in the air, defending her vision of the world and its rightness against his cynical vision of survival of the smartest and the best-prepared. He knew he was right; he'd proved it to himself over and over again, but that didn't stop him from wanting her and wanting what she could give him. He wanted her body, and he wanted her vision. He craved it; like the desire that never left a man to dream himself back to that half-forgotten time when the sun warmed him clear to his bones, when the dust was hot and soft and thick under bare feet, the sky was wide enough to dream all day in and the fishing was always good in the long, green, hot afternoons.

Could she really give him that? He didn't know. But he knew that he'd never wanted a woman more; he'd never tasted sweeter kisses; he'd never felt more right about anything in his life than he did having this woman in his arms.

Justine shuddered as she felt his bare hand warm on her thigh, beneath her scanty nightshirt. She reached up and buried her fingers in Clayton's dark hair, pulling him closer, aching for him with every fiber of her being. How strange that this should happen. How strange that she realized she loved him—just a few short hours ago—and suddenly find herself in his arms, where she'd longed to be for so long. Surely, this *was* a dream; it had to be.

But the drag of Clayton's palm across the taut peak of her breast as he thrust his hand between them, weighing, stroking, teasing, was not part of any dream. He took a harsh unsteady breath and covered her face with kisses as she leaned back, moaning softly, offering her throat to her lover with pure instinct. She trembled as he kissed her throat, as he kissed the pulse at the base of her throat, as his hand impatiently fumbled with the buttons at her breast and as he touched her, finally, touched her satin-soft skin, warm and bare and flushed with passion for him.

Only for him. When she didn't draw away from that intimacy, when her kisses became only more greedy and demanding, Clayton groaned and swept her up into his arms.

In a few strides he was at her bedroom, and he carried her in, leaning back against the door as he closed it behind him, panting. He let her slide to the floor in front of him, slowly, agonizingly, feeling each tantalizing inch of her body against his. Then he held her against him again, pulling her hips in tight against his, his tongue probing deeply into her mouth, meeting, twining with hers. He was going to make love to this woman; he'd waited too long. She was his—*she was his wife.*

The truth of it struck him like a twenty-pound hammer, and he nearly staggered back. God! What was he doing? What was he doing in her room like this, kissing her until he could almost feel their bodies melding perfectly together, skin against skin? How had his shirt come undone, and hers? She fired his blood, but he'd known that long ago, and he'd guarded so carefully against it, for her sake and for his. How had he let himself be swept away now by the strength of his desire for her, by lust, by pure, unadulterated need? He was no teenage boy, a hostage to his hormones. Yet here he was, a few minutes from making her irrevocably his, from taking her, from doing what he'd only dreamed of doing on that long, dark, lonely drive back from the coast tonight, sick with missing her, with hungering for her... telling himself his business was finished in Vancouver and it was time to go home, but knowing otherwise.

"Clayton—" Her voice sounded strangled against his chest where he held her tight against him, his face buried in her soft, fragrant hair, his heart hammering. "We can't—Sylvie's here—asleep...."

Sylvie! He looked toward the big brass bed, the bed where he'd watched Justine sleep, her dark hair spread against the pillow, her open hand against her cheek, the gesture oddly vulnerable and haunting. He'd stood and watched her so many times, just at daybreak, before going out to start his ranch work.

He held her a moment longer, not sure what she was thinking, except that they couldn't make love with Sylvie here. And Tim sick in the room down the hall. He took a deep shaky breath; it was all the excuse he needed, and he, he told himself angrily, was a hell of a coward.

They stood together a moment longer, waiting for their breathing to ease, waiting for their hearts to slow. Then Clayton bent and gently put Justine away from him, holding her by her shoulders. "Get some sleep, Justine," he said gruffly. "I'll stay with Tim."

"But you're tired from your long drive—" she said, her lips feeling like cotton wool as they formed themselves around the words. No one had ever, ever, kissed her like Clayton had.

"I said I'll stay with him," he said, knowing his voice sounded harsh and not meaning it and not being able to help it. She simply nodded, moving away from him toward the bed, not turning as she felt him open the door quietly behind her. He stopped.

"Oh, and Justine?"

"Yes?"

His voice was soft and low and she felt her heart flip-flop inside her chest again. "If you're going to wear a man's shirt to bed, I want it to be mine." And, astonishingly, he'd shrugged out of the shirt he was wearing and tossed it toward her. Then he was gone.

Justine cuddled down beside the sleeping girl, every nerve of her body on fire and aching. Clayton wanted her. Her husband—the man she loved—wanted her. She needed no experience to know what they'd both felt. And there had been no one around, no need to pretend to honor the hands-off clause they'd both signed. This— what she'd felt between her and Clayton—this was real. The ridiculous premise of their negotiated marriage was the part that was unreal.

Sure, they'd signed a legal and binding document. Sure, Clayton could hold her to the terms of their agreement. But did she care anymore? Did he? Was it worth the paper it was written on? She smiled in the darkness, took a deep breath and closed her eyes, hugging his shirt to her body, imagining to herself that it held the warmth of his.

She loved him. It was as simple as that. And, perhaps in time, he would come to love her. Things were different now; the rules had changed. Somehow she'd teach him that he could trust a woman again; she'd teach him to trust her. She had to. Her happiness depended on it.

"Do you miss Vancouver, Justine—I can call you that, can't I? 'Fraid we don't stand much on ceremony out here, m'dear. Where's that man of yours, anyhow? Probably out talking bull with my Albert. Men!" Helga Smythe was a big blond woman with a hearty manner and a booming voice. She was rather incongruously draped in a wild African-print caftan and was swathed in gold chains and bangles, but Clayton had already warned Justine about his unconventional neighbors, a glint of humor in his eye. They had bought up their ranch twenty years before, after a lifetime spent in the glitter of European capitals and had seen no reason to give up the social life and parties they were used to, just because they'd taken up ranching in the Nicola Valley.

Justine smiled and swirled the cold drink she was holding, sending the ice cubes clinking against the thin crystal lip of the glass. "I don't miss Vancouver at all, Helga," she said quietly, smiling at her hostess. "In fact, I feel like I've lived here all my life." It was true; she'd never felt that she fit in and belonged anywhere like she did at Willow Springs.

"Ah, yes. Thank God our Clayton finally— Well, well, here's Bill Sutton!" Justine looked to one side and

smiled at another neighbor Helga had just introduced to
the group—there were about twenty or so neighbors and
friends of the Smythes and Truscotts out here on the
patio. Ah! There was Clayton. He was standing with his
back to her a few yards away, engrossed in a conversation with several other ranchers—probably talking bull,
as Helga had said. But as she watched, she saw him turn
slightly sideways until he caught sight of her and the look
he gave her brought a quick flood of warmth to her
cheeks. She looked away and took a hasty sip of her cold
drink, knowing that Clayton knew perfectly well why she
did it.

It was uncanny how he seemed to know what she was
thinking. He hadn't left her side this evening, although
he'd hardly exchanged a word with her in the car as
they'd driven over. But that didn't surprise her anymore. She was getting used to Clayton's long silences. It
had been a week since the night Tim had had his asthma
attack, and the momentous change in their relationship
that Justine had thought had taken place had apparently been nothing more than a figment of her imagination, or a product of her longing for things to be
different between them. Or had it?

Clayton had ignored her completely until four days
later when she'd picked up Mrs. Grant from the bus de-
pot in Merritt. Then he'd returned to his previous behavior, demonstrating casual affection in public and
leaving her strictly alone in private. At first Justine had
been hurt, and bewildered. And then she'd resigned
herself to this new, more cautious arrangement. After
all, it was plain that Clayton did not want anything to
change between them. Thinking clearly and calmly,
Justine had to concede that that was by far the wisest,
safest course. The last thing Clayton wanted, he'd told

the lawyer, and her, was to get tangled up in an affair with his temporary wife.

Yet sometimes, when no one was around, she'd caught him looking at her in a way that she could not mistake, a way that brought the blood surging to her cheeks, that brought the deep flutter of anticipation in her breast and a memory of the ache inside her that only Clayton could ease. It was hard to describe—it was as though their relations were even cooler than before, but yet at the same time each careful look carried more weight; each glance, each accidental touch held more meaning. It was as though they were more exquisitely aware of each other than they had ever been before, and more aware of the danger.

"So this is the new Mrs. Truscott?" The voice was a little slurred by drink and Justine didn't like the way this newcomer was eyeing her boldly. He looked vaguely familiar, too, but Justine knew she'd never met him before. "Mighty pretty little lady, but then Clayton always did have an eye for a good-lookin' filly."

Justine straightened, a little shocked at the familiarity, but she immediately relaxed when she felt Clayton's presence beside her. He took her hand and tucked her arm into his. Justine automatically stepped closer, feeling the warmth of his body at her side.

"That's right, Willie. I'd advise you to mind your manners when you speak to my wife," he said in a low, dangerous tone that the other man could not mistake. "Justine—meet Willie Merton, Tim and Sylvie's uncle."

"Please ta meet ya," The other man slurred, automatically blinking and nodding and swallowing all at the same time. His pale blue eyes narrowed. "Say—hope ya don't think you're gonna get the kids, Clayton, now that you've fixed yourself up with a quickie wife—''

"That's enough, Merton."

The other man immediately stopped talking, as though some shred of survival instinct had told him that it might be very serious for him, and probably very painful, if he didn't.

Clayton turned smoothly away, putting his back to the man and Justine turned with him. He led the way toward the back of the patio, where a screen of lilac bushes separated the tiled pool area from the more prosaic corrals nearby.

"Willie is one of Angela's brothers. He's some kind of a used car wheeler-dealer from Kamloops these days. Figures!" He frowned, then suddenly grinned down at Justine. "Now tell me the truth—would you buy a used car from that man?"

She giggled and shook her head, her spirits tremendously lightened. She looked up at him, eyes shining in the half light. He looked down at her, his attention arrested on her smiling mouth. He put his arms around her, sliding his hands up under the little bolero jacket she wore. Her shoulders were bare underneath and she shivered.

"Cold?" His voice was very low and suddenly Justine was afraid to look up at him.

She cleared her throat. "No," she said softly. His hands moved over the bare skin of her back, warming her, caressing her, sending the blood pounding through her veins in a sudden mad rush.

"Me, neither," he breathed, his mouth just brushing hers lightly, gently, impossibly erotically. "Me, neither."

And, although she was aching for him to deepen the kiss, he didn't, but with a deep unsteady breath he released her and took her arm again.

"Justine—" he said, when they'd made nearly a complete turn around their hostess' flower garden, rich with scent in the moist evening air, and she'd made a few bright remarks about the roses and said something inconsequential about the nicotiana.

"Mmm?"

"I think it's best this way, don't you?" He looked almost stern and yet she saw the shadow of something very sad in the back of his eyes. She knew what he was talking about—she didn't need to be told that it wasn't about the layout of the garden.

"Y-yes," she said, finally. "I—I believe you're right." But she didn't mean it, not at all.

Neither did Clayton. His feelings for this woman he'd accidentally married were making him crazy. One moment he was wildly angry with himself for even thinking about making love to her, the next he was trying to convince himself that having a short affair with her wouldn't be so bad. He'd be able to extricate himself in the end, he thought—no woman yet had touched his heart. He'd give her pleasure and take pleasure and it would be a fair exchange, agreeable between two adults. Maybe he'd get her out of his system if he made love to her—it was just the artificiality of living with an attractive woman without being able to touch her that was driving him insane.

For a couple of weeks Clayton worked like a man possessed. He got up even earlier than usual, and rode Thunder hard for an hour or two before returning to the ranch for breakfast. He avoided the house in the daytime and worked outdoors until dark, returning for a quick evening meal that he sometimes ate in his office; then he'd work on his books until past midnight. He took more cold showers in that time than he had in his entire life. And none of it made a damn bit of difference. Justine O'Malley Truscott was slowly driving him mad.

Justine tried not to think about what was happening. She knew that she loved this man and that was enough. She put her faith in the power of love. There were nearly three months of her contract still to run and that, she hoped and prayed, was time enough for circumstances to change. Justine trusted her feelings.

Then, one morning very early near the end of July, everything changed between them.

Clayton had gruffly asked Justine at dinner the night before if she'd like to ride out with him in the morning to have a look at one of his bull pastures. He'd noticed her regular afternoon rides, often with one of his top hands, Lance Colman, and had found himself wishing she'd ride with him. It was an annoying reaction—almost a jealous one, he admitted to himself, and it irritated the hell out of him.

Justine, trying to quell her pleasure and surprise at his unexpected offer, had said she would. Mrs. Grant chimed in with her comment that she'd be taking the children to Merritt the next day to visit with her niece and her children, so there was no reason for them to rush back. Justine had been a little surprised—this was the first she'd heard of any excursion to Merritt—but kept her thoughts to herself. Had Mrs. G noticed the new coolness between them and wondered at its cause?

Next morning she scrambled into riding gear—jeans, boots, a cotton shirt, a cowboy hat and a vest to hold off the morning chill—and tiptoed down the stairs. Clayton had already gone out. She found him in the stable, saddling Sissy. Thunder was already saddled and waiting, tied just outside the stable door. The big sorrel danced sideways, and whinnied as she approached, blowing a stream of warm breath toward her.

"Ready?"

Clayton gave a final tug to the mare's cinch and pulled on it, testing its safety, then nodded. He looked askance at the canvas knapsack she carried and raised one dark eyebrow.

"A picnic," she said, blushing a little. "Just a few things." She knew this wasn't a social outing—he only wanted to ride out two or three miles to where some of his prize Hereford bulls were pastured. But when she'd packed the lunch last night she'd been thinking of more—perhaps spending the morning with Clayton. Could it hurt to be prepared?

She smiled uncertainly. Clayton looked grim and a little remote this morning. Perhaps he regretted his hasty invitation of the night before. Perhaps he, like herself, wasn't sleeping all that well these days. But as he casually handed her Sissy's reins, their eyes caught and held and something hidden deep in the blood sprang to life between them. Justine caught her breath, surprised by the sheer unexpectedness and pleasure of it. Then Clayton grinned, and reached up and tweaked her hat down toward her nose and she laughed and suddenly the morning, perfect already, took on even more splendor.

Was that possible? The sun had brushed the dusky hills surrounding the ranch with rose and gold and purple, even though it hadn't arisen fully yet from behind the valley's rim. The sky was already that thin, clear blue that warned her that it would be hot later on. But when

wasn't it in this country? There was dust and heat and
the sharp tang of sage and bunchgrass, and now, as they
rode along a cow trail, the sweet scent of the second crop
of hay, freshly cut in the rich irrigated bottom land, and
waiting for the big baling equipment that would come
later to gather and bind it.

Justine followed Clayton's lead, an easy ground-
covering pace that kept her attention on her riding and
her reins, but allowed her the confidence once in a while
to gaze around, to see the magnificent country through
Clayton's eyes. This was his, as far as the eye could see,
and this had been his, through his pioneering Truscott
ancestors who'd settled the land in 1869, for four generations. It was his legacy and his trust. To a man like
Clayton, there could be no other life.

Justine looked ahead, admiring the way Clayton sat
on his horse, relaxed, easy, as though he and the sorrel
shared the same heart and breath. It was the seat of a
natural rider, she knew, wondering ruefully if she'd ever
ride as well. Not in three months, she thought, biting her
lip and deliberately putting aside the unwelcome
thought.

"How are you doing?" Clayton had pulled up on a
knoll and waited until she came up to him. Her hair was
flying free, most of it escaped from the thong she'd used
to tie it back, and her eyes were shining. He felt the familiar ache inside as he met her smile with a long, level
look.

"Fine!" Sissy snorted and tossed her head and coyly
danced away from the stallion's interested nicker. "How
much farther?"

Clayton tipped down his hat to shade his eyes from the
fresh brightness of the morning sun, now just over the
rim of the mountains to the east. "Oh, another twenty

minutes or so.'' He turned and pointed down the valley. ''The bull pasture's over there and then I've got something else I want to show you.''

''Oh?'' Justine's heart quickened. He wasn't in a hurry to get back to Willow Springs, to get rid of her. ''What is it?''

''A surprise.'' Clayton smiled and nudged Thunder's sides with his knees. The horse was off. Clayton frowned. When had he decided to take her to the springs? About the time, he realized, that he'd finally faced what had stared him in the face for nearly three months now....

They raced the last five hundred yards to the springs. Clayton had pointed out the green patch of cottonwoods and willows on the hillside in the distance after they'd checked on the bulls—massive sleepy-looking creatures that grazed slowly or lay hugely in groups of two or three, chewing their cuds, each looking away from the other, seeming to need to preserve his intense masculine isolation. Justine marveled that they were so quiet and Clayton told her that most bulls got along just fine as long as there weren't any cows around to fight over. And range bulls, he said, were far more placid creatures than dairy bulls or bulls that were kept in barns or corrals.

Then they galloped up to a small knoll on the side of the valley and Clayton pointed out their destination.

''Race you!'' she'd challenged, her eyes gleaming with mischief.

Clayton laughed, feeling something turn slowly inside him. ''To be fair, I'd better spot you a hundred yards,'' he teased, his gaze lingering on her flushed cheeks, her soft laughing mouth. ''I'm riding a champion.'' She'd taken off her vest and tied it behind her saddle and he fought against a sudden desire to reach out and cup the soft swell of her breasts against the thin fabric of her shirt.

"You're on!" Then she was off, and he had a hard time reining in the stallion as it plunged and champed at the bit, scenting a challenge. When Clayton judged she'd galloped about a hundred yards, he gave the big horse his head, with a whispered word of encouragement, and horse and rider were one in this race they couldn't lose.

Justine dared a quick look over her shoulder as she neared the cottonwoods. She'd heard the pounding of hooves hard behind her and knew it was over. Sissy was fast, but Thunder was a proven winner. Clayton shouted something as he drew abreast and she shouted something back, but the sound was lost in the wind. Then he was past her, and she was laughing, her eyes blurred from the wind as she pulled up, her breath nearly gone.

Clayton had already dismounted and he swung her down from the saddle with a whoop and pulled her hard into his arms. Their eyes caught for just a second and then his mouth took hers, hard and possessive, and his kiss took away any breath she had left. She moaned and twisted in his embrace, reaching up to pull him closer, her mouth eager to meet his, her heart pounding against his. Her senses swam with pleasure, but the vital need for oxygen won out and they broke apart, laughing and panting.

Clayton caught up Sissy's bridle and Justine turned from him and walked away, knowing that he would follow. She walked to the edge of the greenness that cradled this spring on the hillside, its icy, life-giving waters springing from the very earth, the source for the creek that ran by the ranch house and that gave the ranch its name. Willow Springs. She leaned against the rough trunk of an ancient cottonwood and waited.

Behind her she heard the faint sounds of the horses as Clayton loosened the girths to let the horses drink briefly, then gave them their heads to crop the soft green grass. For a moment she didn't hear anything more and she tensed slightly, but then he was right behind her and she relaxed again, leaning back against his chest, closing her eyes with the full, secret knowledge of her love for him.

His arms came around her from behind, strong and warm and bare—when had he removed his shirt?—two iron bands of comfort, and then he bent his head and kissed her on the side of the neck. Softly, warmly, deliciously his lips moved slowly down to the sensitive spot where her shoulder joined, and she felt her body shudder with pleasure. Then his hands moved to the front of her shirt and he undid her buttons, slowly, one by one. Justine trembled as his palm curved against the warm skin of her belly and slid lower, to undo the fastening of her jeans. Then he pulled the shirt from her shoulders and dropped it to the grass. Justine gasped as he covered her breasts with his hands, stroking, smoothing.

Still he hadn't said a word and she hadn't seen his face. She felt his breathing quicken as he touched her, and a deep crooning sound arose in his chest behind her head. She felt the sound, rather than heard it and, unable to bear it any longer, she turned smoothly in his arms and pressed her aching breasts against his bare chest and reached up to pull him down to her, greedy for his mouth, for the pleasure only he could give her.

There was nothing between them any longer, could not be. Clayton kissed her deeply, sliding one hand under the denim of her jeans to pull her hips tightly against him. He groaned. He was wild with need for her, she was ready for him and wanted him, too, he could feel it....

Kissing her hungrily, his mouth joined to hers, he lifted her in his arms and carried her to the green shadows of the oasis. Then he sank to his knees and laid her gently on the deep moss. His eyes worshiped her as he pulled her jeans down over her hips and legs, bending to pull off her boots and bending again and again to kiss her soft white skin. Then, eyes holding hers proudly, he stripped and sank down beside her, his blood on fire at the look in her eyes—of joy, of willingness, of innocence. Of love.

"Take off your hat, cowboy," she said softly, and he smiled and sent it whirling into the grass. There could be no waiting now; they'd both waited too long. Clayton kissed her deeply, moving over her almost at once as he felt her urgency, as he felt her thighs part eagerly to welcome him. Then he caught his breath—

"Justine!" he gasped, his voice ragged with the shock of his discovery and the restraint he knew he had to maintain so desperately—especially now.

She felt him freeze and, afraid he would withdraw and rob her yet again of what she wanted as much as life itself, she clenched her hands around his hips. "No!" she gasped fiercely, arching to meet him, refusing to let him go. "Don't—" And then she gasped again, and the question was academic.

Clayton held himself still, trying to absorb the impact of what he'd just learned, trying not to cause her any more pain, cursing himself for not thinking, not even for a moment, that he might be the first lover she'd ever had. That thought brought him up sharply and he was filled with the fierce knowledge that, against all reason, he was glad, that he wanted to be her first lover, and her last. This woman was his. This woman beneath him...

He watched her expression change. First there was surprise at the unfamiliarity, then the shock of discovery as she felt her own body's instant response to him, a response they shared as deep waves of pleasure shuddered through her body and, in the process, nearly snapped his control.

He waited a moment, gritting his jaw with the effort, waited for her to open her eyes and look at him. He had to see her. She was confused, she was a little shy, her eyes were filled with wonder.

"Is that— Oh!" she began, then gasped as she felt him begin to move slowly, deliberately. "Isn't—?"

"That's not all, my darling," he whispered, kissing her deeply while his body began its own rhythm of loving her, of pleasing her, of taking pleasure from her. "It's only the beginning—I promise you." He took a deep shuddering breath as he felt her tentative response and then the world exploded around them both as they clung to each other, fully joined, spirit and body, together as one at last.

Chapter Nine

When Justine opened her eyes—she must have dozed for a while, she thought, close and warm in the arms of the man she loved—she saw her own hand first, spread wide over Clayton's chest as though to touch as much of him as possible, and, on her finger, the smooth brightness of her wedding band.

The morning sun had climbed high and hot in the sky but its clear heat was gentle on her skin through the cool of the lacy green cottonwoods whispering far above them. She lay for a long moment feeling the smooth rise and fall of Clayton's chest beneath her cheek, then lifted her head to look at him.

He wasn't asleep, but was watching her with eyes dark with inner knowledge. They were lovers now, husband and wife, and nothing—*nothing,* she thought fiercely— could take that away from them. From her.

"Happy?" he murmured.

She smiled tremulously and kissed the bare skin of his shoulder. "Happy. Happier than I've ever been before."

With one quick movement, he rolled her over so that he was looking down at her, her dark hair tousled and spread in the grey-green sea of moss beneath her. He felt his blood quicken, in remembrance and in anticipation. What a fool he'd been to think he could get her out of his system like this! What a fool he'd been to have believed—until now—that making love was just good sex by a less honest name. What a fool he'd been to fight against his crazy passion for this woman—the strongest and the most frightening feeling he'd ever had. But fight it he must....

He bent to kiss her softly. "Did I hurt you?" he whispered. "I—I never dreamed that—"

"No," she said, her clear tawny eyes looking up at him, a faint blush staining her cheeks as she remembered. "It was—"

"Beautiful," he finished for her, breathing the word against her mouth. "Simply and completely and totally beautiful. And so are you—"

She reached up to pull him down to her, eager again for his kisses, and neither one said anything more for a long time.

Later, they spread the cloth Justine had brought and shared the picnic from her knapsack—Mrs. G's crusty bread, butter and cheese, tomatoes and herbs fresh from the garden and long drafts of icy cold water from the spring. She felt hungry, and happy, and more alive than she had ever been before. Clayton didn't say much, but his eyes, when they met hers, said everything—he cared for her, he *must*, she thought. After today, surely both

their lives had changed forever. Hers had. She had to
believe that his had, too.

But apparently it wasn't that simple. Yes, Clayton's
attitude toward her had changed but, if anything, he
seemed even more withdrawn. Or perhaps he was just
the same as he'd been before.... Only now, his indifference hurt; it hurt more than she'd ever dreamed it could.

What had she expected? Why, she'd thought it was
simple: he would move into her room and they'd truly
become the happily married couple the rest of the world
believed them to be. What a ninny you are, Justine!
What an idiot—to think beginning an affair with the
man you'd married might amount to anything more than
exactly what it was if you weren't married—just an affair, she thought bitterly to herself a month after riding
out to the bull pasture with Clayton.

But she'd known all along that their marriage was not
a true marriage—never had been, never would be—so
surely Clayton's behavior shouldn't surprise her? If
anything, Justine realized, with a glimmer of hope, she
should be encouraged by his aloofness. After all, a man
who'd embarked on a simple affair would hardly take
the time to maintain such a callous indifference to his
mistress, unless *something* was bothering him a lot.

To Justine's great surprise, for three days after their
return from the spring, Clayton had virtually disappeared. She saw him at lunch twice, but that was it. He'd
barely spoken to her when he did see her.

Then, the fourth night, she'd woken from a dream-
less sleep, sensing a presence in the room and had realized Clayton was there, standing by the bay windows and
staring out into the darkness, his black silk dressing
gown loose on his tall frame. She watched him for a long

time, her heart full, sensing the deep turmoil and unhappiness in him.

"Clayton?" she had said softly, and as he'd turned she'd held out her arms to him and silently he'd come to her bed. They'd made love in a storm of passion, with an urgency and a desperate longing that had shaken her. But never once did Clayton speak. And when she'd opened her mouth to tell him how she felt, unable to keep her feelings to herself any longer, he'd silenced her with kisses.

When she awoke in the gray dawn of morning, her body sated and full, he was gone. He hadn't stayed until morning.

He never would; she realized that now. And the knowledge that he wouldn't stay and share the waking with her, that he would only come to her bed when he was driven to it by his great need, that he couldn't—or wouldn't—talk to her, and her discovery that she needed him as much as he needed her... If he hadn't sought her out, she knew, she would have gone to him. And why not? she thought, with a fierce surge of anger. Yet she felt betrayal like a small deep wound that would not heal. She'd betrayed herself and her principles, and he'd betrayed her, too. And yet she could no more turn him away when he came to her than deny herself breath.

Life at Willow Springs went on, a soothing rhythm broken only by the bitterness of her private thoughts. The children had warmed to her completely, and the three of them spent many long afternoons together, playing, picnicking and reading stories together under the cottonwoods by the weathered rail fence. The children, she thought sometimes, made the long weeks bearable. The children and Mrs. G.

Then, unexpectedly, Justine was called upon to appear at a court hearing. She'd known it was coming, in part by Clayton's increased tenseness and irritability—at least she assumed his irritability had to do with the legal battle over the children—and the long conversations he had in his office with John Stusiak. She knew that one hearing had taken place and this was another one, mysteriously called by the Mertons. Had they changed their minds? Justine thought, with a quick rush of optimism. Gladys Merton had made it clear that she did not really want the job of raising her grandchildren.

When Justine had reported her visit, Clayton had been thoughtful. He obviously hadn't known of the grandmother's genuine affection. But he'd smiled without humor when she'd mentioned the interest of Angela's brothers and sister. He'd expected as much, he'd said; they'd been the main beneficiaries when Angela was alive.

Now, despite Justine's objections—she would have preferred the anonymity of a hotel but Clayton had been curiously adamant—she and Clayton and the children were staying with her parents in Burnaby so that they could attend the early-morning hearing. Justine's parents were thrilled at finally meeting the children.

"It'll be just like when you were little," Mrs. O'Malley had said, beaming, "when you had your friends over to visit." Justine was an only child and she knew her parents had mourned the brothers and sisters who hadn't followed, children with which they'd hoped to fill the rambling old Burnaby Mountain house.

Justine followed her mother to the guest bedroom upstairs, the room she and Clayton were to share—naturally. Justine could think of no likely argument to preclude her sharing a room with Clayton, and she could hardly plead a raging cold or some other virulence at this stage. It would only astonish her mother and perhaps raise questions Justine wasn't prepared to answer. And it was laughable, really, to feel such fastidiousness now. Still, at Willow Springs it was her secret. Here... well, she just wanted to keep some part of her life sacrosanct.

Thank goodness, she thought, pulling a flannel nightie over her head as she got ready for bed that night, thank goodness they hadn't had to spend the night in her old room—the children were sleeping there—the room in which she'd grown up and dreamed her girlish dreams. Having to share her virginal bed with a flesh-and-blood husband of convenience would have been too painful to contemplate.

Clayton was sitting out on the old veranda with her father, each with a beer in his hand, sporadically discussing the kinds of things men discuss on porches in the dark—baseball scores, politics, fishing stories. She hoped he'd stay there until she'd gone to sleep.

No such luck. Just as she reached to turn out the bedside lamp Clayton walked in, shutting the door behind him. He took in her flannel armor in an instant—she could tell by his quickly narrowed gaze—but he didn't say anything. She reached over to his side, turned on his lamp, then moved back and turned her light out. She rolled onto her side, facing the wall, and tried not to listen to the sounds of him undressing, or getting into bed, or the accidental brush of one warm leg under the sheets. Clayton, she was positive, was not wearing pajamas. Somehow, in her parents' house, it seemed vaguely indecent.

"I suppose," came his breath suddenly at her ear, making her start with surprise, "that you think you're invincible in that—that thing." She could hear the trace of cool amusement in his voice.

"I don't know what you're talking about," she replied stiffly, in a fierce whisper. His voice, warm and soft, sent shivers of an excitement she knew only too well down her spine. Damn, damn and double damn that she'd got herself into this hopeless entanglement with Clayton Truscott! Hadn't she been thoroughly warned of the danger—by him, by the lawyer and by her own instincts the moment she'd laid eyes on him?

"You know exactly what I'm talking about," he said. Then, like her, he turned his back to her and moved so that he no longer touched her.

A hot tear trickled to Justine's pillow and she angrily brushed it away. He didn't want her; in fact he acted like he was angry with her for something. Was it her fault they'd been put in the same bedroom? Had she been the one who'd insisted on staying with her parents?

She didn't want him, either! She hated him for what he was putting her through, although she knew he was not to blame. So why, then, did she wish he'd turn to her and hold her and murmur sweet things against her cheek and warm her skin to satin fire with his touch?

"Mrs. Truscott—"

The Mertons' lawyer paused and turned to look at Clayton, sitting beside John Stusiak at a table in the courtroom. Clayton regarded him steadily. The lawyer rocked back on his heels and Justine thought he looked ridiculously pompous and rather suspiciously pleased with himself.

She was in the witness chair and had been duly sworn in although John had protested to the judge that there could be no need for Justine to take the stand at all.

"I don't mind, John," she'd said quietly, touching the lawyer's arm. She had no intention of lying—she'd told Clayton that—and the truth could not hurt Clayton's case, regardless of what she'd be asked. If she could do anything at all to help settle this dispute, she was only too glad to do it.

"Mrs. Truscott," the lawyer repeated, "I just have one question for you and I'd like you to answer it honestly—"

"I object, Your Honor," Stusiak interjected. "Of course the witness will answer truthfully."

The judge agreed and asked the Mertons' lawyer to continue.

"Mrs. Truscott, do you love your husband?"

There it was: stark and cold before her. Before her and a hundred others. Justine closed her eyes for a moment, hearing John Stusiak's objection like a noise through a tunnel in the distance. She'd never dreamed it would happen like this. She clasped her two hands together on her lap, appearing to wait patiently while the lawyers argued the validity of the question before the judge, while in fact she was struggling to focus on the question—and her answer.

"Mrs. Truscott?" It was the calm, quiet voice of the judge, a woman, leaning down to her.

"Yes?" Justine swallowed and looked up.

"I realize the question asked is a rather unexpected and perhaps unlikely one, but counsel for the Mertons has challenged the validity of your marriage although—" Here she consulted some papers on her desk through a pair of reading glasses that hung from a black cord around her neck. Justine had a sudden flash of the horn-rimmed spectacles she'd worn to get this job in the first place, nearly five months ago—it seemed so much longer. Another deception; her life was filled with so much deception and subterfuge these days that it made her heart ache. "—I see here that there's absolutely no question of the legality of your marriage.

"I think, though," the judge continued, leaning down again and smiling reassuringly to Justine, "that the question ought to be answered, since it clearly has some bearing on this case which is, above all, to consider the welfare of the children. Do you love your husband, Mrs. Truscott?"

She didn't dare look at Clayton before she answered. She wet lips that felt dry and looked steadily into the eyes of the judge. "Yes," she said quietly and firmly. "I love my husband very much."

There was a stir in the area where the Mertons were sitting and Justine inadvertently glanced over, catching Gladys Merton's bright look of approval in a sea of whispers from her husband and her grown children, Natalie Ransom among them. Then she looked at Clayton and her heart froze.

He was looking at her with such a cold, level look of disgust that Justine nearly cried out. His jaw was tight, his eyes were black with anger and she knew then that he thought she was lying.

"That will be all. Thank you, Mrs. Truscott." Justine barely heard the judge's words, as she returned to her chair beside Clayton, her legs unsteady, thankful for John's solicitous hand on her arm. She took her seat stiffly, conscious of the rigidity of Clayton's thigh beside hers. She was aware of her husband's icy fury, as no one else in the courtroom was, and suddenly it took every shred of strength she had left to stop from bursting into tears.

* * *

"You're looking a little peaky, Justine," Mrs. Grant said, bringing another basket of plump red ripe tomatoes over to the scrubbed wooden table in the kitchen. "Why don't you take a nap? I'll finish these up. You might not get another chance once Clayton brings the children back."

"I'm fine, Mrs. G," Justine replied, her feet tucked up around the rungs of the stool. She frowned slightly. It was true; she had felt unusually tired these days—and had for a couple of weeks now. She'd felt especially bone weary since the hearing ten days ago, but that was probably due to a little depression, as well. Clayton still hadn't heard the judge's decision, and he was behaving like a bear with a sore paw around the house these days. He rarely spoke to her and when he did, she ached at the coldness and indifference in his eyes. He hadn't touched her, either. Even the "public affection" he'd been so clever at had been dropped. Perhaps he felt it didn't matter any longer—everything depended on Judge Hanratty's decision now, expected any day. Certainly he'd never come to her bed again. Could what they'd shared really have meant as little as that? Could she have been so very, very wrong?

Justine straightened and sighed, feeling the tension in her lower back. The two women had spent the morning putting up peaches and now they were tackling the bushels of tomatoes that had come in from the ranch garden. Mrs. G swore there was no substitute for home-canned tomatoes in the dead of winter. Not that Justine would be here to find out....

"Tell me what the children's mother was like, Mrs. G," Justine said with casual interest. She wanted to divert her gloomy train of thought and realized that the housekeeper had been discussing the Merton clan for the past five minutes. Angela and her role in the tangled affairs of the Truscotts had always intrigued her.

Mrs. Grant gave her a bright, perceptive look and shook her head. "That one was always trouble, I can say that. I take it you've heard the rumors?" She didn't wait for Justine's acknowledgment. "I suppose you have. You've been here long enough, and there's plenty only too willing to spread gossip."

What was Mrs. G hinting at? "I've heard a few things," Justine admitted nonchalantly.

"You've probably heard that Angela and Clayton were seeing each other before Lyndon proposed—that's the usual story that gets around, that the Truscott brothers scrapped over her and Clayton lost out—" Justine looked up, aghast. She'd never heard anything of the sort.

The little housekeeper snorted. "Harumph! As if she was worth fightin' over! Not a jot of it's true. I know. I knew them two boys better than anyone on God's earth and poor Lyndon was dotty over that woman and Clayton didn't have the time of day for her. Saw through her, he did, right from the start.

"Trouble was, Angela couldn't take no for an answer. She'd been spoiled rotten since she was a little girl and had her heart set on marrying one of the Truscotts. Poor Lyndon was wrapped around her little finger—always had been—but that wasn't enough. She set her cap at Clayton. If she couldn't have Clayton, she'd do her darnedest to make trouble for him and take Lyndon as second best."

Trouble? "Some folks around here believe that malarkey about Clayton and Angela but anyone with the gall to mention it when I'm around gets set straight soon enough! No matter what mess of lies that woman cooked up about my Claytie, I know it ain't true. Trouble is, Clayton was too much the gentleman to put her down in public back then and now it's too late. Talk spreads and pretty soon folks believe it 'cause they've heard it so often.''

Clayton and Angela? His brother's wife? Did that account for his cynicism about women and his belief they were only after what they could get? Justine shook her head, confused.

"Believe what?"

She met the housekeeper's surprised stare with an inquiring look. Plop! The last tomato went into the quart jar and she pushed it down gently, absently noting how much like blood the fresh tomato juice looked against her skin, the tomatoes feeling still half-alive and warm from the sun.

"Why, that Tim is Clayton's son, that's what.''

Justine made an exclamation and her paring knife clattered to the table.

"Oh dear! Did you cut yourself? Here's me talking and you listening and neither one of us paying attention to what we're—''

"No—it's nothing, Mrs. G.'' Justine tried to smile reassuringly, but she knew she wasn't succeeding very well. She rinsed her hands at the sink and held them up. "See? Just tomato juice.''

She wiped her hands carefully, feeling a little as though she was seeing everything through the wrong end of a telescope. Her heart was hammering like a rabbit that's run too far already, but has no course left but to run on. Her knees felt shaky and she wanted to sit down. Tim—Clayton's son!

"I just wanted to set you straight, dear, because I knew you'd hear talk around the valley. But you can put your mind at ease. There's not a word of that nonsense that's true—I'd stake my life on it. Sure, Tim looks like Clayton, but he takes after his daddy, too. They're all Truscotts, ain't they? It's just this guardianship business has got people talking again...." She looked fierce for a moment, then her face softened as she took in Justine's pale, strained features.

"Clayton's no saint—I know you're aware of that—but he's a one-woman man, through and through. He's not an easy man to know—I guess you realize that, too—and he keeps his feelings to himself. Always has. But I've known him since he was a little boy and one thing's plain as day—" Mrs. Grant hesitated, and fixed Justine with her direct, honest gaze. "He loves you, my dear. I thank God every night for that miracle, 'cause after what happened with his brother, Clayton swore he'd never let himself get trapped by a woman like Lyndon did. And he's stubborn, too—oh boy, don't I know it!"

Then Mrs. Grant had insisted she go upstairs to rest and had shooed her from the kitchen with motherly noises and warm, knowing glances.

What had that been all about—Mrs. G saying it was time enough and looking enormously pleased? Justine yawned and put her feet up on her bed and closed her eyes.

Clayton and Angela.... She wasn't sure what she felt, but how could she be jealous of a dead woman? And Mrs. G had been so sure it was all just gossip anyway. The children's mother sounded like a very mixed-up, unhappy person, someone who needed sympathy more than condemnation. And as for Clayton loving her...

Justine winced at the sheer physical pain that wrenched through her at the thought. Obviously their charade had been a success so far, if even Mrs. Grant had been taken in by it. Lord, she was weary....

She frowned again. What *had* Mrs. G been hinting at in the kitchen? Time enough for what?

Justine's eyes snapped open and she stared at the ceiling aghast. My God! She fumbled in her bag for a calendar she kept in her wallet and studied the date, counting back the weeks with an ominous feeling. She'd never been regular and perhaps that's why she hadn't been concerned, but surely... They'd taken precautions, at least since they'd made love that first time on the hillside.

But they hadn't then. And it would be a miracle indeed if a new life hadn't been created out of their passionate coming together that morning at the spring.

Justine buried her head in her arms and bent over, as though in pain. Oh God! She was pregnant. What was she going to do now?

Chapter Ten

Justine leaned back against the gray roughened trunk of the old cottonwood, absently breaking the petals from a daisy with her fingers. Sylvie had brought her a bunch of field daisies, buttercups and purple vetch a little earlier, and then had scampered off to play with her new kitten, the kitten Clayton had brought the children a few days ago and which had become Sylvie's inseparable friend.

She'd had a few days to think over her situation and come to grips with it. After her first feeling of utter horror at how wrong things had gone, she'd felt a fierce outrush of protective emotion and tenderness toward her unborn baby. She'd checked with Dr. Crisp—just to be sure—and had sworn him to secrecy, telling him she wanted to wait a little before telling Clayton.

Then each night, she'd studied her options over and over into the wee hours of the morning before finally coming to a decision. Clayton would hear about the custody settlement any day now; she'd leave shortly after. It was going to be hell to leave the children, but there was no other choice and she had an agreement with their uncle to fulfill. Clayton didn't really want her—he'd made that plain enough in the last couple of weeks, and she had a little pride left. Sure, she'd made a mess of things: she'd fallen in love with her employer, she'd allowed herself to begin an affair with him, she'd been naive enough to end up pregnant.... But she could salvage something—her pride, at least.

She'd go back to Vancouver as she'd originally planned, buy the MacAllister House, start the play school—perhaps with a partner, maybe Gwen—and somehow she'd manage. Lots of single mothers did, with fewer advantages than she would have. Of course, eventually she'd have to tell Clayton about his child. But not now, not when her heart was so grievously wounded, not until the magic of time had helped heal her and she could face up to his indifference. He didn't want a child, and he didn't want a wife—he'd always made that clear—and there was no way she'd risk telling him now and have him insist on continuing their marriage.

He would, too. She knew he'd never shirk what he saw as his responsibility and she knew a man who'd fight that hard to keep his brother's children would never let his own child go. But she couldn't bear to live with that option: perhaps he felt nothing for her now, but at least he hadn't grown to hate her for trapping him in a marriage he didn't want.

Where had Sylvie gone? Justine looked around with faint alarm. "Tim!" The boy was constructing a dam on the shallow creek that ran through the bottom of the garden—the creek that had its source at the hillside spring—and she had thought Sylvie was there helping him.

"Yes?" Tim stood up, his hands muddy to the elbows, his face shining with his engineering triumph. "C'mere and look at my—"

"Have you seen Sylvie? Is she there?"

"No." The boy looked around, unconcerned. "She was here a minute ago, playing with Kitten. I—"

Justine got to her feet, looking around. No little girl. Could she have gone back to the house? Mrs. Grant was baking this morning and... Suddenly her heart leaped to her throat.

There, way over by the stock corrals she saw the gleam of a coppery head. Sylvie was climbing into the corral! And there were a hundred half-wild range steers in that paddock, waiting for the liners that would take them to the auction later that afternoon.

Justine threw down the mutilated flower she still had in her hand and broke into a dead run, shouting over her shoulder for Tim not to leave the yard.

It seemed to take forever to reach the log corral.

"Sylvie!" There she was—trotting unconcernedly after her kitten, calling to it in a high-pitched voice while the kitten scampered this way and that, batting at the little swirls of dust it raised with its quick playful evasive rushes.

And not forty yards away from the little girl, at the other end of the paddock, was a wild-eyed herd of jumpy cattle, bawling and milling indecisively. She had to get Sylvie out of there! Without a second thought, Justine ducked between the rails and climbed in after her.

Clayton frowned as he impatiently touched his heels to the big sorrel's sides, absently feeling the surge of power as the stallion responded, drawing on the reserves of stamina that made him the best stud Willow Springs Ranch had ever produced and the best cutting horse Clayton had ever had the pleasure of breaking.

He was tired—they were both tired—and he was sweaty and hot and dusty and he felt like hell. He'd left the ranch this morning, long before Justine had awoken—he could still see the curve of her cheek as she'd lain there, turned away from him in sleep, and he could still feel the struggle he'd had with himself just to stand there, not to bend down to kiss her soft lips, to touch her once again.... When he'd left, he'd thought he'd only have a couple of hours' work ahead of him. But some fences were down that shouldn't have been and he'd been chasing runaways for the past three hours. He'd missed his lunch and he hadn't bothered to wait for breakfast and he felt as though he hadn't slept for a week....

Dammit. He hadn't, either. He couldn't get Justine's pale face out of his mind, or the hurt in her eyes when she looked at him. Clayton set his jaw in determination. It was for the best; he had to do what he'd done for the sake of them both. It was no good; he never should have gotten involved with her. Involved, hell! He was so tied up and tangled up inside that he was beginning to wonder if he'd ever be able to cut her out of his life without bleeding to death himself. This is what had happened to Lyndon, and, by God, he wasn't going to let it happen to him. He'd fight it with everything he had. With everything four generations of stubborn, hardheaded, independent-minded Truscotts had given him.

He never should have made love to her. A virgin! It wasn't just a simple, ordinary, garden-variety affair—it couldn't be to her, and it wasn't to him, he'd discovered. He'd been shaken by the storm of feeling she'd aroused in him, by the strange and tender desire to protect her, to please her, to keep her safe from hurt. And then he'd been the one to hurt her after all, he thought grimly.

He'd made no promises—he'd told her the truth, right from the beginning. That, he told himself stubbornly, was good enough. She had a crush on him; that's all it was, all it could be. She felt she owed him something because he'd been the first . . . and, maybe, that he owed her.

God, what a mess! If only that damned judge would make up her mind and they could both get clear of this. It had to be what she'd want now. The sooner the better. She'd been hurt and humiliated—he knew by the way she looked at him. And he, he swore softly and thoroughly and crudely to himself, was the biggest damn coward and sorriest excuse for an honorable man who'd ever been born in the Nicola Valley. She'd get over it—in time. Would he?

Clayton frowned again, a little uneasily, and urged Thunder on. He was in a hurry to get back to the ranch. He had work to do. Then there were those market steers to load this afternoon. . . .

What was that? He squinted into the distance as he came over a rise and saw the ranch spread out below him. Sounded like something was bothering those steers. And why were they bunched up like that, at the far end of the paddock?

Then his quick scan of the corral took in the situation and he dug his spurs into Thunder's flanks, sending the surprised stallion from a near standstill to a furious gallop. God! What was Justine doing? Didn't she know she could get killed in there? A flood of rage swept over

Clayton, rage mixed with terrible fear. He'd never felt terror before. Never. But it had him by the throat now. If anything happened to Justine.... He couldn't let it; he couldn't even bear to think about it....

So far Clayton had not seen Sylvie, but now he did. He saw Justine yell something to her as she raced across the corral and the little girl screamed and ran toward the fence. The steers were nervous and had that plunging indecisiveness that Clayton knew preceded a stampede. Sylvie climbed back outside the corral and Justine followed her to the fence and then, to his utter amazement, he saw Justine turn back into the corral.

"Get out of there, dammit!" he yelled at her and she turned, startled. Just then the kitten, which he saw now, scampered straight toward the steers, then veered off to the left and climbed a corral post, hissing and spitting with annoyance. The tiny kitten's rush was all the spooky cattle needed to set them off.

In slow motion, almost like in a dream, Clayton saw the leaders roll their eyes and begin to run, the rest plunging behind, mindless and implacable, a mighty wave of pounding hooves and flashing horns. And Justine—dear God in heaven!—had fallen somehow and was lying motionless right in their path.

Thunder couldn't clear the fence; there was no way. But almost before he'd slammed to a halt outside the corral, Clayton had vaulted over the top pole from the saddle and hit the ground running. He couldn't carry her out of the way in time; the thundering herd was too close. There was only one thing to do.

Clayton whipped off his hat and waved it, yelling and moving his arms up and down. The only hope was to split the stampeding cattle into two streams. He stood over Justine's prone, motionless body like Hercules at the gates. He'd protect her or he'd die trying.

For one awful moment, Clayton didn't think it was going to work. He knew a runaway herd would avoid an obstacle if it could—like a boulder or a tree or a man on horseback. He'd challenged a stampeding herd on horseback before and it wasn't a pleasant feeling. He'd never done anything this crazy before.

But it worked. Just as it seemed that he could almost feel the hot breath of the crazed steers, the leaders hesitated and swept to either side. For an eternity—it couldn't have been more than ten or fifteen seconds—the dust roiled around him, choking and blinding. Then they were past.

Clayton heard the yells of some of the men as they arrived to help. One threw open a gate to the next paddock and the frightened cattle plunged through the opening. Suddenly, there were men on horseback and men with ropes. One ranchhand scooped up the sobbing Sylvie and another plucked the complaining kitten from the fence post, the cause of all the trouble, and gave it to the tear-stained girl.

Clayton knelt in the dust. He felt for Justine's pulse. It was strong. He ran his hands lightly down her limbs, feeling for injuries. Nothing broken. But there was a nasty bruise at the back of her head—he could feel the thick lump—and he sent up a quick prayer that that was all that was wrong with her.

"Gosh, boss—you all right?" It was Lance Colman. The cowhand looked pale under his leathery tan. "And the missus?"

"I'm okay, Lance." He grimaced as he lifted Justine in his arms, as gently as he could. "You take Sylvie up to the house and tell Mrs. Grant to call the doc. I'll take care of my wife.''

Clayton looked down at Justine's pale, dust-streaked face. *I'll take care of my wife,* he'd said. He'd done a hell of a poor job of it so far. *My wife!* He knew then with a deep surge of feeling, as though a great river had broken its bonds somewhere inside him, that that's really what she was—*his wife*—no matter what was on some foolish piece of paper that they'd both signed. She was his wife, truly his wife. And he loved her.

His own face was pale under his tan as he looked down at the woman cradled in his arms, taking care not to stumble in riding boots that had not been made for walking. Maybe it was too late. Maybe he'd fought against his feelings for her too long. Maybe he could never repair the damage he'd done.

He swept into the house with her, past the horrified Mrs. Grant and the sobbing Sylvie and the pale Tim who had come in to see what all the commotion was about. He laid her carefully on the sofa and stood back, breathing hard, his face grim. Mrs. Grant bustled around, removing Justine's boots and loosening her blouse and gently wiping the dust streaks from her face with a damp cloth.

''I'll get an ice pack for that bump on her head,'' she said to Clayton, giving him a quick look of concern. Clayton hadn't moved; he just stared down at Justine with a look of raw pain. ''Don't worry, Clayton, she'll be all right—you'll see. She's got a nasty bump but she'll come to in a minute. Wh-why don't you go up and change?'' This last was said tentatively as the tall, brooding man she'd helped raise and loved like the son she'd never had gave her a long look and raised one arm to wipe his dusty brow. It was a look that needed no words and the little housekeeper felt her heart soar despite the worry over Justine. She knew he wouldn't leave his wife; he wouldn't leave her ever again.

But when the doctor arrived, Clayton did leave, just long enough to take a quick shower and change. If Justine had to go to the hospital—and Clayton wanted her completely checked out for injuries—he was going along.

At the hospital he alternated between standing at the window and staring out grimly, his hands gripping the window frame so tightly his knuckles showed white, and sitting at Justine's side, gently stroking her brow, holding her hand, talking to her in a low voice. He'd held her in his arms all the way into Merritt in the back seat of the doctor's car, unwilling to trust anyone else near her and unwilling to wait for the ambulance that Dr. Crisp had suggested calling.

"Looks like just a bump, but we can never be too sure with head injuries," the doctor had confessed to Clayton after checking Justine over carefully. "And I don't like the way she's not regaining consciousness. I'd feel better if we could take a few X rays and keep her under observation overnight."

The doctor also had checked Sylvie over thoroughly and other than a few scrapes and exhaustion caused by all the excitement, the little girl was fine. When they'd left the ranch house, she was curled up asleep in a big chair in the kitchen, thumb in her mouth, her kitten snoozing peacefully beside her.

"Clayton..." Clayton wheeled from the window and crossed the room to the hospital bed in a couple of strides. Justine's eyes were still closed, but she had a slight frown on her face. He bent to kiss her and her eyelids fluttered open.

"Yes, darling?"

It *was* Clayton; she'd thought she'd heard his voice reaching through the long darkness of her sleep. She frowned again. *Darling?* So they were back to that, were they? Public affection. Where was she anyway?

"I'm, uh... Where's Mrs. G?" she whispered.

Clayton rang the buzzer to call a nurse. "You're in Merritt, sweetheart. In the hospital. Don't you remember what happened at the corral?"

"Corral? Oh..." Memory dawned and she closed her eyes again. The corral, and the kitten, and Sylvie.... She'd fallen somehow. Her left hand instinctively went to her flat belly under the white sheet. What if...? She licked dry lips. What if something had happened to...?

Dr. Crisp came in, all efficiency, and began taking her pulse and blood pressure. He told Clayton that the X rays had shown no fractures and he was sure it was just a case of slight concussion and that in a couple of days she'd be right as rain.

"You've got a strong, healthy wife, young man," he said with a smile. "Take more than a knock on the head to put her out of commission."

"Baby...what's happened to...?" Justine licked her dry lips again. She couldn't say it, but she had to know.

"Baby?" Clayton frowned. "Sylvie's fine, Justine. Not a bruise. And so is the kitten—" He laughed, wanting to see her smile, but she didn't smile. She just looked at him with those big dark eyes and he felt the pain of the way he'd hurt and betrayed her like the twist of a knife in his heart. "Sylvie's fine, darling. It's you we're worried about now." He hated the sound of his own voice.

But she was looking up at the doctor, the question still looming in her eyes.

"Fine, Justine," he reassured her softly. "Nothing to worry about. The baby's fine."

And the fear went out of Justine's face as she closed her eyes in relief. Thank God! If they'd just leave her alone—all of them—just leave her alone. She was so tired . . . so very tired.

Clayton frowned—he'd just told her that, hadn't he? He gripped the window ledge again while the doctor finished his examination. He should tell her—now. He should tell her that he loved her and didn't want her to leave Willow Springs and the children—and him.

He turned, but something in the calm, level gaze she returned held him still. Perhaps he shouldn't—not now. Not when so much had happened. He'd tell her later, when she was back at the ranch, when she was stronger . . . when they could be alone again.

Clayton Truscott had never known a moment of indecision in his life before, but he was afraid now—afraid of committing his feelings to her, afraid of her scorn, her possible denial, of her referring him to their agreement—the wretched agreement he'd insisted upon all those months ago.

What if he was wrong about her? What if she didn't feel the same way about him? He'd never hesitated to take a firm course of action in the past, no matter what the difficulties. But nothing he'd ever taken action on before had mattered so much. He had to talk to her—soon. But he had to be sure; he had to do it right.

A couple of days later, when Justine finally made her wobbly way down the staircase into the living room of the big ranch house, a little pale still, but determined—he could see that, and his heart swelled with love for her—the decision was taken from him. She told him quietly, with no visible emotion, that she would be leaving as soon as he heard about the settlement of custody.

"What do you mean—leave?" He felt like he'd been kicked in the gut. Didn't she see how things had changed now? How he hadn't left her side for days? Couldn't she see how much she meant to him? Suddenly he was angry. "You can't leave."

"I certainly can—and I will," she said calmly, her chin rising. Only her eyes betrayed surprise at his vehemence. "I intend to be out of here just as soon as you hear that your case is settled."

"Your six months are not up," he said flatly, instantly regretting it when he saw her jaw tighten. Why had he said that? He hadn't meant to remind her of their marriage contract. At this point he wanted to forget the idiotic thing had ever existed. All he wanted was for her to stay. If she walked out now...

"As soon as you hear the judge's decision, my part in this—this farce is over," she said, her hazel eyes flashing and only the slightest quaver in her voice betraying her inner emotion. "Whether I've been here six months or not is immaterial. I'm leaving."

He studied her a moment, his face impassive and his blood boiling. It took every ounce of control he had to keep his voice level and stop himself from stepping forward and shaking her. "Why are you telling me this now, Justine?"

"Because I wanted to give you a little notice, Clayton," she replied scornfully. "In case you wanted to manufacture an appropriate story so we could feed the children a few more lies!" He flinched. He felt her contempt like a physical blow.

"You knew this was all necessary—don't pull the innocent act on me now, Justine," he said coldly. "We have an agreement. And I intend to hold you to it."

"Hold me to what?" she cried suddenly, her hard-won calm fractured beyond repair. "Our agreement was broken long ago, when I went with you to the—the spring! That wasn't in our agreement—" He had gone white and she faltered. This was killing her—to have this out with him now. Why couldn't he have just let her go? Quietly? Without a fuss?

She trembled and leaned against the banister and closed her eyes. She still felt terribly weak. Maybe she shouldn't have come down now to talk to Clayton, but she'd heard Mrs. Grant go up to her room an hour ago and she wanted to inform him of her decision here, on neutral ground, not upstairs in her bedroom where all she wanted to do was open her arms to him and welcome him to her bed again.

"I thought you wanted it as much as I did," he said quietly. "If you blamed me for breaking our contract, why didn't you tell me about it before this? Why didn't you claim the compensation that was rightfully yours?"

Justine cringed at the bitterness she heard in his voice. Why hadn't she? Because, of course, she *didn't* blame him. Of course, she *had* wanted him as much as he'd wanted her. But she couldn't tell him that, could she? She'd tried to, in the courtroom that day, but then he'd looked at her with such bleak anger that it had almost destroyed any belief she had left in the power of love. People who cared about each other didn't behave this way toward each other.

She turned to go, keeping her head down. This had been a mistake, coming down here to tell him. She was so tired. She wouldn't say any more. He knew what she planned to do now. She would keep her end of the bargain—she owed him no explanations. Clayton suddenly stepped forward and grabbed her arm. She looked up, startled, and saw the flash of pain in his eyes.

"Don't look at me like that—like you're afraid of me," he growled. "Not after what we've had together." It hurt him to see the bruised, frightened look in her eyes. Dear God, what had he done to her—the woman he loved? "Answer me, Justine—why didn't you claim your compensation?"

"Because I—I didn't want to hurt you," she whispered, truthfully, "or your chance with the children. And—" she had to tell him "—because I didn't blame you. You're right, Clayton, I wanted you as much as— as—"

Roughly he hauled her into his arms and bent his head, crushing her mouth with his. He kissed her hungrily, angrily, nearly smothering her with his demand that she respond, that she kiss him back, that their powerful need for each other burn away everything else between them. Like it had so many times before. But she couldn't, she wouldn't; she was just too cold inside.

She forced herself to remain stiff in his embrace, repulsing him even while she felt the liquid flame of his touch trickle treacherously through her veins. Of course she wanted him; of course he could make her want him. But it solved nothing between them, nothing at all. Finally, with an oath, he thrust her from him, his eyes blazing.

"All right, Justine," he got out roughly, closing his eyes for a split second as he fought to regain control. "You win. Leave if you want. I won't stop you."

Win? What a laugh, she thought, almost hysterically as she climbed the stairs slowly, clinging to the handrail. There were no winners here, only losers—her, the children, their unborn child, even Clayton ultimately. She knew he would regret not knowing his child, but she couldn't help that, either. A child deserved a whole mother or father to love him, not two unhappy parents who stuck together out of some twisted notion of duty.

She paused as she heard the telephone ring in his office and turned. Could that be John Stusiak? Calling at this hour?

It was. Holding her breath, she heard Clayton's terse replies, knew that the news was positive and suddenly felt her own troubles lift for the moment. This was such good news! It was what Clayton had wanted so desperately. She silently crept back down the stairs and went through the half-open door of his office.

"Clayton?" He was slumped in his chair, his face buried in his hands. But he raised his head at her soft inquiry. She caught her breath at the bitter resignation she saw on his face. "I—I couldn't help but hear. It's good news, isn't it?"

He laughed, a short harsh sound that held no amusement. "I guess you could say that, Justine. I have custody of the children, if that's what you mean. And I've got you to thank for it, I understand."

"What do you mean?" Justine felt bewildered, both with his attitude and the biting sarcasm of his remark.

"John says you swung the case in my favor at the hearing. When you said you loved me." Her heart ached at his bitter smile. "Thanks, Justine. I owe you. I never asked you to lie for me."

She stared at him, aghast. He thought she'd lied at the hearing! He could believe that—of her? There was no hope left anymore, no hope at all. There never had been;

she'd only deluded herself. There was no point in even telling him he was wrong.

With a small inward moan of agony, Justine fled up the stairs. Tomorrow, just as soon as Clayton had left the ranch house for the day, she'd be gone. She never wanted to see him again.

Chapter Eleven

For once, events conspired with her.

Justine awoke later than she'd planned, exhausted by the paroxysm of weeping she'd finally allowed herself when she went to bed. But even while she wept, she had clenched her fists and punished her pillow mercilessly. Damn him! Clayton Truscott wasn't worth crying over! Finally she'd fallen asleep out of sheer exhaustion, glad that he hadn't come up yet. He had to pass through her bedroom to reach the room he slept in and she didn't trust herself not to fly at him with tooth and nail if she saw him again.

When she got up, Clayton had already left the house. And Mrs. Grant had left a note on the breakfast table saying she'd taken the children into Merritt to get new shoes for them and to do the grocery shopping. Justine couldn't help the wave of cowardly relief that swept over her. What was she going to tell the children? It killed her to have to leave them like this, after what they'd already been through, but there was no help for it. This way—it was a coward's way out, she knew—she'd leave them an ambiguous note and let Clayton do the explaining.

It didn't take long to pack. She was leaving everything that had been bought with Clayton's money—the silky dresses, the hand-tooled riding boots he'd given her, the matched set of luggage they'd used on their honeymoon at Whistler. Ha! What a farce this business had been, from beginning to end.

But it wasn't over; it wouldn't ever be, even if she left this morning and never saw Clayton Truscott again. His child was growing inside her at this very moment; a child conceived in love—at least on her part—and conceived in very definite unarguable legal wedlock.

Justine looked down at the ring on her finger and pulled it off. She held it in her hand for a moment, turning it over and over, then left it on her carefully made bed. It sat on top of the folded Cowichan sweater she'd finally finished knitting for Clayton, winking brightly in the morning sunshine. The knitting wasn't the best job in the world, but the sweater was completed and would show him that she meant what she'd said.

Then her luck ran out. Mrs. Grant had taken Clayton's Jaguar since the station wagon she used was in the repair shop getting new brake pads. She'd forgotten about that. Justine had felt no compunction about using Clayton's car to get to the Merritt airport. Desperate circumstances required desperate solutions. That just left her the ranch Jeep, a rather ungainly open-air vehicle that was reliable but slow. And it seemed to have about a million gears, most of which she managed to grind when she drove it.

Justine set her jaw and tossed the single bag she'd packed into the back seat. She'd driven the vehicle over

the hills before, when she'd taken coffee out to the
ranchhands who'd been branding a few miles away at the
community pasture. It would have to do. She jumped
into the front seat, took a deep breath, looked quickly
once around the ranch yard, full of old-fashioned
blooms and peace and greenery, a place where she'd once
felt as if she belonged, then bent and turned the key in
the ignition.

Dependably, the ancient vehicle roared to life.

"You carry on, Lance—I've got something back at
the ranch I've got to do." What made him turn back
when he did he never knew, but Clayton suddenly pulled
up Thunder and shouted a few instructions to the cowhands with him before wheeling and heading back to
Willow Springs.

His mind was in a turmoil this morning. Spending the
night on the sofa in his office hadn't helped—but he deserved it. It was part and parcel of the stubbornness that
had almost blinded him to the reality of exactly what it
was he was doing. What he was doing to Justine and
what he was doing to himself.

Lyndon's marriage had been a mistake—but that
didn't mean he had to make the same mistake. How
could he compare the grasping, conniving woman his
brother had married with a woman who'd picked out a
sweater kit when he'd told her, quite seriously, that he'd
buy her anything she wanted in the entire town of Whistler? Had it been a test? An unconscious one? If it had
been, he despised himself for his insufferable arro-
gance. At the time he'd derived a certain cynical pleasure out of making the offer, but he didn't think Justine
had taken him seriously at all. Now that he knew her

better, he knew she hadn't. No, Justine wasn't Angela. She wasn't like any woman he'd ever known.

And besides, Clayton thought, his lips twisting with painful memories, no matter how it had seemed to him, he knew that Lyndon had been happy in his own way. His brother had loved Angela. For all her faults—and she'd had plenty—he'd loved her. At least Lyndon had had that.

Frowning, Clayton urged the stallion on. He'd been pigheaded and stubborn and too quick to take offense with Justine, but if he could right that now, he would. Even if she turned him down flat—and he deserved that, too—he had to take the chance. He couldn't live with himself if he didn't.

At least they'd be alone and could have it out completely this morning. Mrs. Grant had taken his car to town and that left Justine without wheels. His grim satisfaction when he'd learned that this morning had long since evaporated. He'd had to convince himself he was angry with Justine. It wasn't true—he loved her, and if he was angry with anyone, it was himself.

As he came over the rise that showed him the ranch spread out before him, a sight that never failed to fill him with pride in his accomplishments and the accomplishments of the men and women who had gone before him, Clayton suddenly had an unfamiliar feeling of unease. The ranch house had that too-silent look of desertion. No one was there; he knew it in his bones. He looked at the open doors of the garage. Damn! The Jeep was gone.

He wheeled Thunder and scanned the horizon, his eyes narrowed and his hat pulled low against the sun. She couldn't have gotten far; he could still see the haze of dust hanging in the air just where the road rounded the flank of the hill and followed its curves to the main highway.

He'd cut her off. She wasn't going to get away from him, not now! Clayton leaned low on the big sorrel's neck and whispered words of encouragement. He was depending on the quarter horse to show his stuff and he had no doubt the stallion would deliver. This was one race Clayton meant to win.

As the horse flattened out, sending up a plume of dust beneath his pounding hooves, Clayton couldn't help but grin a little at the thought of her taking out the rattle-trap Jeep. You had to hand it to her—she had plenty of pluck and was determined as hell.

But so was he. Dammit, so was he.

Justine thought it was thunder rumbling in the hills in the far distance at first. She glanced to the south but the sky was a pure, clear blue—no sign anywhere of a summer storm.

She wrestled with the thick steering wheel, trying to avoid a gaping pothole. Wham! She felt like her bones were being jostled out of their sockets in the old Jeep. It certainly hadn't been built for comfort. Why hadn't Clayton ever bothered to get this road fixed? Perhaps if she slowed down.... Justine let her foot off the accelerator slightly and the engine slowed. So did the vehicle. At this rate she'd be lucky if she made the main highway before Mrs. G was due back.

Irritated, Justine reached up to push a strand of hair from her face and just caught sight of a plume of dust from the corner of her eye. She turned her head to the right in disbelief, nearly dislocating her shoulder as the Jeep's right wheel caught and grabbed at a pothole.

It was Clayton, riding like a madman across the valley flats toward her! She could see great patches of sweat darkening the sorrel's bright sides and felt her heart begin to pound. He was trying to cut her off at the next curve.

Panicking and cursing the road, the Jeep and her delayed departure, she rammed the accelerator to the floor and winced as the engine whined in protest. It was no use, she thought, nearly weeping with exasperation as she pitched from side to side, trying to control the steering wheel. This vehicle was not built for comfort, but it wasn't built for speed, either.

Clayton was nearly to the road now and she heard him shout. She wouldn't answer. There was nothing he could do. He might be able to catch up to her, but she wasn't interested in anything he might have to say and he couldn't stop her, either. She was leaving—she had left, she corrected herself—and there wasn't a darn thing he could do about it.

"Justine!"

She kept her attention fixed on the road in front of her. "Road" was stretching the meaning of the word considerably.

"Justine! Stop for a minute. I want to talk to you!"

She ignored him, carefully gearing down to negotiate another rough patch.

"Dammit! Listen to me, Justine!"

"No!" she shouted back, turning her head to see that he'd nearly caught up to her and was racing Thunder along the ditch beside the road. "I've listened to you long enough!"

"Where are you going?"

"I'm leaving—what does it look like?" The wind in her eyes and her hair whipping across her face had made her vision blur. She raised one arm to wipe her sleeve across her eyes. Damn the man anyway! Why did he have to do this to her?

"You can't leave, Justine—"

"Watch me!"

"What—what about the children?" Hell! This was not coming out like he'd planned. Why was she arguing? Why didn't she stop that stupid vehicle and listen to him like a civilized woman would? Of course, him chasing her down on his horse wasn't exactly the action of a civilized man.

"I—I'm sorry about the children but I..." He couldn't catch the rest of her answer, but she showed no signs of slowing.

"You can't just leave like this!" he shouted, leaning forward urgently, "The children need you!" His heart failed him as he saw a smooth stretch coming up and saw her shift into high. She wasn't stopping. And he couldn't ask much more from the exhausted animal under him. The woman he loved was driving that broken-down Jeep right out of his life. Just like that.

The children need you! Justine choked back a sob as she stepped on the gas and realized that Clayton had pulled up behind her. It was killing her to do this to him, but she had to. Tears that she could no longer blame on the wind streamed down her cheeks. He had given up. He was letting her go. Then the great cry came from behind, the cry she'd never thought she would hear.

"*I* need you, Justine!"

It echoed around and around her, a great full-hearted cry from the heart. Could she have heard right? Had Clayton Truscott really said what she'd thought he'd said? Gradually she let up on the accelerator until the vehicle slowed, then stopped in a choking cloud of dust. She couldn't even see him behind her anymore.

Wearily, as though it took every ounce of energy she had left, Justine opened the door of the Jeep and got out. There was no point in even trying to turn the unwieldy vehicle around on this narrow road. She began to walk back. He'd said he needed her—she had to find out what he meant.

Clayton saw her slow and his heart stopped. He held his breath, not daring to hope.... Then he gave a great whoop and urged the tired horse on. He met her halfway and swung out of his saddle.

"Justine—" His voice was hoarse. She looked up at him, the first hope he'd seen in her eyes for weeks. He stepped forward, suddenly awkward. "Justine, I—" Then he took her in his arms and held her tight, bowing his head into her hair, drinking in great lungfuls of her fragrance, closing his eyes, feeling her bones against him again, so fragile, so precious, so strong. He'd come so close to losing her! God! It scared the hell out of him to think how close he'd come... He'd been so stupid—so incredibly stupid.

"Justine—look at me—" He held her face between his two hands and his piercing blue gaze burned into her eyes. "I love you, Justine. I love you and I—I don't want you to go. Ever!"

"Oh, Clayton...." Her eyes filled with tears all over again. Could this really be true? Could she be dreaming after all? "I—I can't believe that—"

"Yes! Yes, my sweet darling—believe it," he said, bending to brush her lips lightly with his. "Believe it because it's true," he whispered against her mouth. "I love you." And he took her in his arms again and kissed her properly and she kissed him back, with the hunger that they'd both denied for so long. And Thunder, after waiting patiently for a time, began cropping grass along the roadside, taking a well-deserved rest.

On the long slow walk back to Willow Springs, hand in hand, with many pauses to hold each other and to kiss each other and to tell each other how much they loved each other, Clayton told Justine all about Lyndon and Angela and the gossip over Tim. He told her how Angela had shown up at Willow Springs once after Clayton had been away for a while, tending to some of his other business, and how she'd sobbed on his shoulder about some injury or indignity, real or imagined that she'd suffered. He'd just had to put down one of his favorite brood mares and he hadn't been feeling too hot himself at the time. They'd shared a bottle of whiskey and somehow—Clayton grimaced when he told her this and Justine could see how much it still bothered him—they'd ended up in bed together. At least, he said, when he woke up next morning with a splitting headache and a world-class hangover, she was in bed beside him. He never knew if he'd made love with her or not—he thought not, considering his condition and the fact that he'd never been attracted to her. But she had said he had and he hadn't denied it. It went against his code of honor to dispute something like that with any woman, even if she was no lady, and he *had* been in bed with her. In his mind he was guilty.

Then, when he'd found out Lyndon planned to marry Angela—he hadn't even known his brother was serious about the flighty neighbor girl they'd both known all their lives—he'd intervened, urging his brother against it. He felt her behavior with him was an indication of her character and he'd wanted to protect his younger brother, without providing the details of how he knew.

Lyndon had been enraged at his interference and had gone ahead with the marriage.

"Then I found she was funneling money to her brothers in Kamloops to put into some of their get-rich-quick schemes and keeping Natalie supplied with cash—she hadn't married Philip at that time—" he said with a quick glance at Justine. She thought of what Mrs. Grant had told her.

"When I confronted Angela with the evidence and asked if Lyndon knew about it she told me that Tim was my child and if I so much as breathed a word to my brother, she'd tell him everything. Well, she had me." Clayton's eyes had that cold look of anger that she'd remembered so well when she'd first met him. But when he turned to her and smiled, the anger melted away and she could only see the pain. "I couldn't take that chance," Clayton went on softly. "Lyndon already hated me for trying to stop his marriage and—"

He sighed and stared down at the dusty road, absently kicking at a rock—a rock she seemed to remember very well bouncing over in the Jeep. "I never found out the truth, Justine. Was she lying? I don't know—she lied about everything else.

"I wish I knew—but I don't," Clayton finally concluded, his eyes bleak with the pain he'd never shared with anyone before. "And I wish I'd mended my fences with my brother, but I didn't.... And now, with them both dead..."

Clayton turned to her and Justine put her arms around him. He smiled, a rueful sort of self-mocking smile that melted her heart, and he touched her cheek lightly with the back of one hand. "I'm afraid you're not getting much of a bargain, sweetheart—a man with a past he's not proud of and stubborn as hell to boot."

"I don't care what's happened in the past! The only thing that matters to us is the future," she whispered fiercely, her heart overflowing with love for this man who loved the children, and her, so much. "We can thank Angela for one thing at least—we have Tim and Sylvie."

She leaned her head against his broad chest and stayed there for a long moment, feeling the hot sun on her back and the strong, steady thud of his heart under her cheek and the solid strength of his arms around her. How lucky she'd been, that the Fates had brought this man to her, this true-hearted man. Perhaps now was the time to tell him....

"Clayton—" she began shyly, stepping back and taking his hand in hers. She placed it on her belly and held it there. His eyes widened at her action and she blushed a little. "I'd planned to tell you this sometime anyway—even if I left—and, well, I hope you won't mind but..."

"You're going to have a baby." His voice was soft and full of wonder.

"Yes," she whispered, looking up at him, then went on timidly, "Do—do you mind?"

"Mind?" He laughed, a shaky sort of husky laugh. "My darling—I thought I was the happiest man in the world when you stopped that Jeep. Now I'm even happier—if that's possible." He held her and kissed her and Justine's heart nearly exploded with happiness at the love and joy and pride she saw in his eyes. How could she have thought for a moment that this man would not want a child of his own? It was just that he was so sure he'd never find a woman he'd want as a mother for his child. And now he had her.

When they got back to the ranch, Clayton handed Thunder over to a stable hand with instructions for someone to pick up the Jeep and went into the house with Justine. She went to the kitchen counter, where she'd left the note for Mrs. G and the children, and ripped it to pieces. Thank goodness, they'd never know.

Clayton pulled a bottle of champagne from the refrigerator and reached up for a couple of glasses. Then, with a proud smile and a tender look at her, he put the champagne back and pulled out a bottle of sparkling sweet cider.

"Sit here, darling," he said with a grin, waving her to the window seat. "I'll be right back." She heard him take the stairs by twos and smiled happily, her hand on her still-flat midriff, her eyes on the gentle green cottonwoods rustling outside the window. She wouldn't have to leave Willow Springs after all. She'd live here all her life and help raise Tim and Sylvie and their baby... and maybe more. They'd become part of that unbroken chain of strong hardworking people who belonged to the Nicola Valley.

She looked up expectantly. Clayton had returned. He held up two pieces of paper. "Yours... and mine." He gave her a copy of their contract. Laughing together, they ripped it to shreds and dropped the pieces in the cold kitchen wood stove. It would be kindling for the next fire.

"And I saw the sweater you finished, up on our bed." He grinned, and she smiled back, liking the way he'd said "our" bed. She'd never wake alone again. "No one's ever done anything like that for me before. Thank you—" He bent to kiss her. "I knew I hadn't married a quitter when I watched you struggling along with that.

I'll wear it with pride." He grinned, and she laughed, blushing a little with pleasure.

Then his eyes burned into hers, and she felt her heart turn over with joy at the look in his. "And something else, my love, before we celebrate our future." He held out his hand, reaching for her left one.

"Will you wear this ring again, Justine O'Malley Truscott," he said solemnly, holding her gaze with his, "as a symbol of my everlasting love?"

"I will," she said, simply and clearly, and he slid the ring back on her finger. She closed her fingers around his tightly and leaned forward to kiss him. How close they'd been to losing it all!

"And now," Clayton said, smiling and popping the cork with a flourish and pouring the pale yellow liquid into two heavy crystal stemmed glasses that had belonged to another Truscott woman before her, "to us, my beautiful bride. To public affection—" she laughed, and held up her glass to his "—and to private satisfaction!"

And they both drank to that.

* * * * *

Silhouette ⚭ *Romance*®

COMING NEXT MONTH

#826 STING OF THE SCORPION—Ginna Gray
Written in the Stars!
Jake Taggert was a true Scorpio—intense in all his passions, and when he saw a chance for vengeance—he took it. But Susannah Dushay was nobody's victim and *Jake* was about to be stung!

#827 LOVE SHY—Marcine Smith
Social worker Jill Fulbright knew all about the agony of shyness—she hid her own by helping others. But eccentric inventor Daniel Holiday's diffidence gave her confidence—even when it came to love....

#828 SHERMAN'S SURRENDER—Pat Tracy
Big-city businessman Jared Sherman refused to succumb to Green River's small-town charm—or its charming librarian—until Amelia Greene unveiled her plan to force his surrender in the battle of love!

#829 FOR BRIAN'S SAKE—Patti Standard
When teacher Bethany Shaw accepted a position as nanny to Mitchell Hawthorne's son, she hadn't expected to fall for them both. Soon, Beth wanted to give Mitch lessons in love—for *her* sake....

#830 GOLD DIGGER—Arlene James
Professor Meyer Randolph didn't want his father's money—he wanted his nurse! Elaine Newcomb's bedside manner made his temperature rise. *Was* she a gold digger... or just pure gold?

#831 LADY IN DISTRESS—Brittany Young
Lovely widow Shelby Chassen wasn't about to chance love again, but Parker Kincaid wouldn't let her go. The powerful attorney melted her icy defenses, saved her life... and stole her heart....

AVAILABLE THIS MONTH:

#820 PILLOW TALK
Patricia Ellis

#821 AND DADDY MAKES THREE
Anne Peters

#822 CASEY'S FLYBOY
Vivian Leiber

#823 PAPER MARRIAGE
Judith Bowen

#824 BELOVED STRANGER
Peggy Webb

#825 HOME FOR THANKSGIVING
Suzanne Carey

Take 4 bestselling love stories FREE

Plus get a FREE surprise gift!

SILHOUETTE®
OFFICIAL SWEEPSTAKES RULES

NO PURCHASE NECESSARY

1. To enter, complete an Official Entry Form or 3"× 5" index card by hand-printing, in plain block letters, your complete name, address, phone number and age, and mailing it to: Silhouette Fashion A Whole New You Sweepstakes, P.O. Box 9056, Buffalo, NY 14269-9056.

   No responsibility is assumed for lost, late or misdirected mail. Entries must be sent separately with first class postage affixed, and be received no later than December 31, 1991 for eligibility.

2. Winners will be selected by D.L. Blair, Inc., an independent judging organization whose decisions are final, in random drawings to be held on January 30, 1992 in Blair, NE at 10:00 a.m. from among all eligible entries received.

3. The prizes to be awarded and their approximate retail values are as follows: Grand Prize — A brand-new Ford Explorer 4×4 plus a trip for two (2) to Hawaii, including round-trip air transportation, six (6) nights hotel accommodation, a $1,400 meal/spending money stipend and $2,000 cash toward a new fashion wardrobe (approximate value: $28,000) or $15,000 cash; two (2) Second Prizes — A trip to Hawaii, including round-trip air transportation, six (6) nights hotel accommodation, a $1,400 meal/spending money stipend and $2,000 cash toward a new fashion wardrobe (approximate value: $11,000) or $5,000 cash; three (3) Third Prizes — $2,000 cash toward a new fashion wardrobe. All prizes are valued in U.S. currency. Travel award air transportation is from the commercial airport nearest winner's home. Travel is subject to space and accommodation availability, and must be completed by June 30, 1993. Sweepstakes offer is open to residents of the U.S. and Canada who are 21 years of age or older as of December 31, 1991, except residents of Puerto Rico, employees and immediate family members of Torstar Corp., its affiliates, subsidiaries, and all agencies, entities and persons connected with the use, marketing, or conduct of this sweepstakes. All federal, state, provincial, municipal and local laws apply. Offer void wherever prohibited by law. Taxes and/or duties, applicable registration and licensing fees, are the sole responsibility of the winners. Any litigation within the province of Quebec respecting the conduct and awarding of a prize may be submitted to the Régie des loteries et courses du Québec. All prizes will be awarded; winners will be notified by mail. No substitution of prizes is permitted.

4. Potential winners must sign and return any required Affidavit of Eligibility/Release of Liability within 30 days of notification. In the event of noncompliance within this time period, the prize may be awarded to an alternate winner. Any prize or prize notification returned as undeliverable may result in the awarding of that prize to an alternate winner. By acceptance of their prize, winners consent to use of their names, photographs or their likenesses for purposes of advertising, trade and promotion on behalf of Torstar Corp. without further compensation. Canadian winners must correctly answer a time-limited arithmetical question in order to be awarded a prize.

5. For a list of winners (available after 3/31/92), send a separate stamped, self-addressed envelope to: Silhouette Fashion A Whole New You Sweepstakes, P.O. Box 4665, Blair, NE 68009.

PREMIUM OFFER TERMS

To receive your gift, complete the Offer Certificate according to directions. Be certain to enclose the required number of "Fashion A Whole New You" proofs of product purchase (which are found on the last page of every specially marked "Fashion A Whole New You" Silhouette or Harlequin romance novel). Requests must be received no later than December 31, 1991. Limit: four (4) gifts per name, family, group, organization or address. Items depicted are for illustrative purposes only and may not be exactly as shown. Please allow 6 to 8 weeks for receipt of order. Offer good while quantities of gifts last. In the event an ordered gift is no longer available, you will receive a free, previously unpublished Silhouette or Harlequin book for every proof of purchase you have submitted with your request, plus a refund of the postage and handling charge you have included. Offer good in the U.S. and Canada only.

SLFW·SWPR

SILHOUETTE® OFFICIAL SWEEPSTAKES ENTRY FORM

4-FWSRS-3

Complete and return this Entry Form immediately – the more entries you submit, the better your chances of winning!

■ Entries must be received by **December 31, 1991**.
■ A Random draw will take place on **January 30, 1992**.
■ No purchase necessary.

Yes, I want to win a FASHION A WHOLE NEW YOU Sensuous and Adventurous prize from Silhouette:

Name _____ Telephone _____ Age _____

Address _____

City _____ State _____ Zip _____

Return Entries to: **Silhouette FASHION A WHOLE NEW YOU,**
P.O. Box 9056, Buffalo, NY 14269-9056   © 1991 Harlequin Enterprises Limited

PREMIUM OFFER

To receive your free gift, send us the required number of proofs-of-purchase from any specially marked FASHION A WHOLE NEW YOU Silhouette or Harlequin Book with the Offer Certificate properly completed, plus a check or money order (do not send cash) to cover postage and handling payable to Silhouette FASHION A WHOLE NEW YOU Offer. We will send you the specified gift.

OFFER CERTIFICATE

Item	A. SENSUAL DESIGNER VANITY BOX COLLECTION (set of 4) (Suggested Retail Price $60.00)	B. ADVENTUROUS TRAVEL COSMETIC CASE SET (set of 3) (Suggested Retail Price $25.00)
# of proofs-of-purchase	18	12
Postage and Handling	$3.50	$2.95
Check one	☐	☐

Name _____

Address _____

City _____ State _____ Zip _____

Mail this certificate, designated number of proofs-of-purchase and check or money order for postage and handling to: **Silhouette FASHION A WHOLE NEW YOU Gift Offer**, P.O. Box 9057, Buffalo, NY 14269-9057. Requests must be received by December 31, 1991.

ONE PROOF-OF-PURCHASE

4-FWSRP-3

To collect your fabulous free gift you must include the necessary number of proofs-of-purchase with a properly completed Offer Certificate.

© 1991 Harlequin Enterprises Limited

See previous page for details.